SUSIE'S SCARE

Susie Cotting thought Lex Maceul was the one and only boy for her. But when he was away doing his National Service with the RAF, he suddenly stopped replying to her letters . . . Two years later, Susie is focused on her own life: working in her mother's shop and taking evening classes. She's convinced herself she's over her heartbreak. Then Lex comes back on two months' leave — and Susie discovers she isn't over him at all!

ADELAIDE JOLLEY

SUSIE'S SCARE

Complete and Unabridged

LINFORD
Leicester

First published in Great Britain in 2017

First Linford Edition
published 2020

A catalogue record for this book is available
from the British Library.

ISBN 978–1–4448–4518–1

Published by
Ulverscroft Limited
Anstey, Leicestershire

Set by Words & Graphics Ltd.
Anstey, Leicestershire
Printed and bound in Great Britain by
T. J. International Ltd., Padstow, Cornwall

This book is printed on acid-free paper

1

Glancing up from his newspaper, Bernie Cotting gave Susie a tender smile. 'Take care, love.'

'Will do, Dad.' Susie bent down and gave him a reassuring peck on the cheek. 'Last week we all decided to go to the cinema to see *Gigi* afterwards, remember? I'll get the ten-thirty bus home.'

Bernie looked at his watch. 'You'd best be on your way if you want to catch the six-twenty bus.'

Susie grinned. It was the same every Wednesday when she went to her evening class. It was the light-hearted repartee that drew them closer together and reminded them to keep up the pretence about her going to a flower-arranging class as her mum, Gwen, thought. As Mum was allergic to flowers, the charade was easy to keep up because Susie couldn't bring her work home.

When Susie had first told her dad what she wanted to do, he'd shaken his head.

'I don't know, love . . . Mum will be worried sick about you doing something like that. Why not take up flower-arranging instead?'

'No,' Susie had responded with resolution. 'It's what I want, Dad. My mind is made up.'

Her dad had angled his head in a quizzical way.

'Has anything happened, love? Anything that's made you want to go to such an extreme?'

Susie's stomach had clenched as an unfathomable icy feeling seeped through her. Her voice however, remained calm. 'No.'

His eyes had searched hers. 'You would tell me, wouldn't you? If something untoward caused you to make this decision, that is.'

'Yes,' she'd said, forcing the icy

feeling to an impenetrable part of her brain. 'Of course.'

Her dad had nodded. 'And you haven't told Mum about it?'

'No, I wanted to talk to you first.'

'I don't like keeping secrets, but keeping them from Gwen is worse.' He'd sighed. 'But in this case, I'll make an exception.'

Susie understood. She also knew Dad was right — Mum would worry herself sick. There was a bit more to it than that, however. Mum owned and ran the local corner shop and before long the whole area would know exactly what Susie — who worked with her mum in the shop — was doing on Wednesday evenings!

'We'll have to keep quiet about it in general. The fewer who know, the less chance she has of finding out.'

Dad had reluctantly agreed.

'If it's what you want,' he sighed. 'Although I can't imagine why a girl wants to learn such things. But yes, you have my blessing.'

3

* ⋆ ⋆ ⋆

Adjusting the large collar of her dolly-mixture-blue coat with a deft flick, Susie stood up and, steadying herself so her body moved with the rhythm of the bus, caught hold of the overhead hand rail and began making her way along the top deck to the steps.

Her stomach was still churning, so taking care not to trip over in her kitten heels she picked her way cautiously along the uneven floor.

What was Lex doing at the bus stop?

Now she was being silly! She saw exactly what he was doing! He was looking into the eyes of a spectacularly beautiful, fashionably dressed girl with perfect Hollywood-blonde wavy hair. Her pink lipstick was starkly visible under the nearby street lamp, and from the way she gazed up at Lex it was obvious they weren't waiting for a bus. Susie's heart lurched as her mind reverberated with the shock of seeing him after all this time — as large as life and twice as handsome — just as the bus she happened to be on slowed down before lumbering onwards.

She knew Lex and his companion had no intention of getting on the bus, even if the bus driver hadn't immediately realised that.

It had been just over two years since she last heard from Lex . . . just over two years since Patsy, his sister, told her in no uncertain terms that she, Lex, and her parents Ted and Beattie Maceul, wanted nothing more to do with her or her family. At the time Susie had pleaded to know what they'd done wrong and begged to know how to put things right.

'You're nothing but trouble, Susie Cotting!' Patsy had thrown at her. 'You and your family think you're the bees' knees, but you're just small-time shopkeepers! It may have been great in your Nan Hetty's time, but you'll go under when those new supermarkets come to Wynnton. Leave us alone and leave Lex alone, too — he hates you and doesn't want to see or speak to you again!'

Lex, who until then wrote loving letters several times a week since going into the RAF to do his National Service, never wrote again.

Susie's stomach knotted now because Lex saw her too — as the bus trundled past the shelter he looked up, and their eyes locked for an infinitesimal second that felt like an eternity!

The look he gave her was nothing short of a bolt from the blue, for instead of animosity in his handsome features, as she imagined there might be if they ever met up again, there was a fleeting affectionate appreciation there instead.

'Willbob Street corner!' the bus conductor called as Susie reached the bottom stair.

'Thank you.' In spite of her churning stomach Susie remembered her manners and smiled. 'I really appreciate you getting the driver to stop right outside my road.'

The conductor grinned. 'It's the least I can do — my missus will be relieved I didn't let you off at the stop on your own at this time of night.'

'That's very kind of you.' Susie was also relieved she didn't have to get off the bus and come face to face with Lex and his stunning girlfriend. 'I'm not usually this late. None of us expected the film to go on for so long. Even the coffee bar we usually go to was shut.'

'These pictures are getting longer and longer,' the conductor smiled.

The whole class she attended finished earlier to see the musical *Gigi*. It was a wonderful film starring Leslie Caron, a rather dishy Louis Jourdan, and the mature but handsome Maurice Chevalier. And until seeing Lex, the magical tunes were still gliding through her mind.

The bus doors slid open, and Susie stepped onto the dark pavement. The bus moved off leaving behind an eerie, creepy blackness. Feeling ruffled, she shivered and although there wasn't a car or a soul in sight, she crossed the road to Willbob Street with vigilance. Looking straight ahead, she kept her stride steady while at the same time treading on tiptoe to prevent her heels from clicking on the pavement.

A small wobbly light suddenly began flickering behind her and Susie's heart almost stopped beating! Her breath caught in her throat like barbed wire and her neck prickled. Stopping abruptly she turned round. Nobody she knew would be out this late, would they?

'Susie,' a soft reassuring voice called through the darkness.

'Dad! Whatever are you doing out at this time of night?'

'I came to fetch you from the bus stop,' he said, dismounting from his bicycle. 'When I saw the bus go right by I wondered where you'd got to. Then I saw it slow down in the distance and saw the conductor drop you off at our street.'

The instant he mentioned the bus

shelter, Susie's stomach started churning — he must have seen Lex with his girlfriend.

'Did you enjoy the film, love?'

'Yes, it was lovely. Gigi was bold and brave and wanted something different.'

'Something different?'

'Yes, Gigi lived in the age where the only real option for women was to find a rich man. Gigi was being trained for the role of — ' She stopped. This wasn't a subject she expected to be telling her father about.

He looked behind himself, looking preoccupied.

'Dad what is it?' Of course — he must have seen Lex and the girl in the bus stop. 'I don't mind,' she said softly. 'In fact it was to be expected, wasn't it? And it doesn't really matter.'

Susie knew in her heart that wasn't true. Seeing Lex looking into the eyes of a stunningly beautiful girl mattered very much. Yet it shouldn't. Two years was more than enough time to get over someone who didn't want you. She thought she was over it. She thought she'd forgotten the way he looked just before her kissed her; thought she'd forgotten how his gentle breath caressed her face; thought she'd forgotten that moment when her eyes closed as his lips met hers; thought she'd forgotten how her knees went weak as he held her close. Most of all, she really thought she'd come to terms with the whole Maceul family hating hers!

Now though, the question arose again. What had her family done to his to turn Patsy against her in such an unexpected and vitriolic way? She and Patsy had been best friends since the age of three — 'joined at the hip' was the expression used to describe their friendship — yet two years ago Patsy turned on her, declaring an end to their friendship. Why?

★ ★ ★

Attempting to control his hammering heart and curb the foolish euphoria blossoming within him, Lex turned to his companion and tried concentrating on her instead.

He was less accepting of Gloria's wheedling tone now than when they met. At first her coaxing baby-voice was amusing and attractive, made him feel masculine and needed. Now, though — especially after that fleeting glimpse of Susie, the first sighting of her in two years — he realised it had grated on him for a while now.

It had taken him over a year to stop thinking of Susie as his one and only after she stopped writing to him. Even after finding out from Patsy that she'd been seeing Tom Prand, one of the guys in the gang Patsy hung around with, he still couldn't stop remembering the silky feel of her of skin, the delicate scent of her perfume as she put her face against his, or how when her fingers inspected the shortness of his hair after he started his National Service, he tingled all over at her gentle touch. He couldn't stop dreaming of a future together.

The worst thing, though, had been the long, lonely months waiting to hear from her and not knowing what had happened. Since then he'd berated himself time and time again for sending that letter asking her to marry him. Then he'd learned from Patsy that Susie had ditched him for Prand — one of those quiffed-up teddy boys who appeared to do nothing in their spare time but hang around being intimidating — wounding him more deeply than he could have imagined.

After all their plans and hopes for their future together, she hadn't even had the decency to tell him herself. Once, when wanting to surprise her while on unexpected leave, and knowing she was with Patsy, he'd gone out looking for her at the local recreation ground. As he peered through the trees just by the entrance he'd seen the gang pushing and shoving each other — except for Prand, who had his arm wrapped round Susie's shoulder.

Too hurt to confront her, Lex had sloped silently away and took Patsy's previously stridently delivered advice to leave well alone.

Tom Prand, of all people! Ever since Prand's stepdad John Magower was promoted to manager at the new gasworks Tom thought he was a big shot! Apart from his National Service Tom never had a regular job. He was an 'iffer and butter', as Lex's mum Beattie had said — someone with high aspirations but no real work ethic.

Occasionally Lex wondered if they were all a bit hard on Tom. After all, his real dad died in 1944 serving King and country in the war. That must have had a negative effect on a young lad, surely? Lex's heart had lurched. Perhaps Susie was what Tom needed to bring him up to scratch? No, he didn't want that agony all over again.

Yet when Susie saw him at the bus stop, she was the one who looked hurt. Her eyes had met his only briefly, but it was a look that would stay with him forever.

'It's here, darling — oh!' Gloria stamped her foot in what she obviously believed was a feminine, charming manner. 'I can't bear leaving you.'

'You must.' Lex forced a rueful smile.

She reached for him. 'But you look as if the world is on your shoulders, darling.'

He wished she wouldn't call him darling. His conscience instantly jabbed at him. He was initially flattered by Gloria's enthusiastic interest in him, and although he had thought he might fall in love with her, given time, after seeing Susie he now knew that was never going to happen.

'You have your exams, Gloria. If you don't go to work tomorrow you won't get to go on that course and all your hard work will go to waste.'

'But darling,' she whined. 'What good is being a personal secretary in the MOD going to do me in the long run?'

That surprised him.

'I thought you were a career girl?'

She sighed. 'I was.'

The taxi driver finally got out of his cab.

'Miss Gloria Adams?'

'Yes,' Lex replied before Gloria denied it.

'Oh Alexander, darling,' Gloria pouted, running her fingers down the front of his shirt. 'Isn't there anything you might like to ask me before I go? Six weeks is such a long time to be apart.'

'We were apart when you went away on holiday a couple of months back,' he reminded her.

Giving her a brief peck on her forehead, Lex opened the taxi door and gently but firmly propelled Gloria through.

As she turned to wave he mouthed a genuine, 'Good luck for your course,' and watched the taxi until it turned right and disappeared.

★   ★   ★

'What don't you mind, love?' Susie's dad, Bernie asked as they rounded their closed-up corner shop. 'What's to be expected?'

They had passed their own front door that went directly onto the pavement to go the back way so her dad could check on his van parked behind the shop before putting his bicycle in their yard shed.

Their shop, right next door on the corner, still called *Hetty's* after Susie's grandmother, had once been a house like all the others in the street.

That shop was Nan and Grandpa's first home. Times were tough then and although Susie's grandpa worked hard as a goods-loader at the local railway depot, it was still difficult financially after Gwen came along. It was then that Nan had started in a small way by baking bread.

'It had to be the best bread around,' she said, 'I was up before dawn so the smell wafted out to those going to and from work on their night or day shifts.'

She shook her head as if not quite believing her own success. 'When I started making cakes to order, things grew from there. After we added the new kitchen with the bedroom above, we made the front parlour into the shop.'

It was a success story Susie had heard many times — still would be hearing if Nan was still alive.

Susie and her dad lapsed into silence as they walked quietly into the dense, foreboding blackness of the back alley past the dark open yard at the back of their shop to their back gate. The cobbled alley was creepy with its line of foreboding brick walls, and was unnerving after dark. Unless she was with someone, Susie always used the front door at night.

She inwardly trembled, and her thoughts instantly returned to Lex. She'd never felt this way about the alley in those days. It wasn't scary then. Her stomach lurched. What had gone wrong between them? No — she mustn't think about Lex!

As Bernie opened the gate, their glowing kitchen light threw a golden shaft of light over their yard and made the area less threatening.

Trying to brush aside all thoughts of Lex, Susie unconsciously shivered.

'That was a shiver-and-a-half, love. The alley can be rather daunting at night. I'm thinking of having one of those new security lights put up so there's a beam when anyone goes by.'

Susie opened the shed door and he put his bicycle inside. Her stomach knotted. Was he going mention seeing Lex?

'There's been another raid,' Bernie whispered as he came out. 'It was in Newynn rather than Wynnton though. At about ten, the police reckon.'

This was one of several raids in eighteen months. Shops broken into — totally ransacked, and the till contents stolen — yet nobody heard or saw anything until the raid was over.

Bernie motioned her towards the back door.

The previous time the family had heard about such an occurrence was the following day when the whole street was full of the news. The raids that seemed to take place at about ten, usually on a Wednesday night, were horrible. Stealing money was one thing, but vandalising was another. The shop owners arrived to find total chaos with stuff broken and thrown around all over the place.

'How bad was it?' she asked.

'It's only Susie and me, Gwen,' Bernie called as he picked up the kettle. 'I'll make us a drink while I'm here.'

He came back from the living room where Gwen was watching the television and lowered his voice as he told her, 'Your mum's really cut up about it, as whoever did it must have come into the shop yesterday or today. That means we're not only implicated, but the police think it could happen to us too.'

Susie got that icy sensation again!

'At least we live next door, so we'd hear it going on.'

'That's true, but the police said whoever's doing it is getting more daring. The culprits might even be capable of a more serious attack if they were disturbed.'

Taking the cups from the cupboard, Susie realised her hand was shaking.

'How awful,' she murmured trying to hide her distress. 'To think that there's someone like that in our midst.'

Bernie inclined his head to Gwen again.

'Shhh, don't let Mum hear you say that.'

Susie nodded, and walked into the sitting-room and kissed her mum. 'How's Mr Rowe?'

Gwen sighed. 'Looking forward to moving into their bungalow on Monday.'

Relieved not to have to mention the attack to her mum, Susie nodded. 'It'll be good for them, but I'll miss them.'

'Yes, me too.' Gwen smiled mistily.

At least her dad had not mentioned Lex.

2

Susie smiled as Mrs Rowe let her into the flat above the shop the following morning. 'Morning, Mrs Rowe. How's Mr Rowe?'

'The same, ducks.'

Mr Rowe had been ill for as long as Susie could remember — a combination of complaints caused by various ailments. His lungs were injured by gas during the first World War, then he'd gone down the mines, and worse still, their only child, an adored son, had died at seventeen years old.

A deep and unexpected memory suddenly swirled through Susie the second she thought of Alfie . . .

No! She mustn't think of Lex and the Meccano Set! An excruciating pain engulfed her. She didn't need memories of their love, their plans, their kisses! She didn't need the imprint his gentle expression left in her mind when their eyes had met at the bus stop.

Crushing all thoughts of him, she dragged her mind back to the Rowes.

It was Mrs Rowe who kept them going when things got rough, especially when her husband was too ill to work. Years ago, people fended for themselves or went into the Union House. Mrs Rowe worked long hours doing every odd job she could. It wasn't until Nan employed her to do some cleaning that she learned of their plight. The Rowes were living in horrible conditions, occupying a tiny room in a damp tenement block where five large families shared one outside privy and one squalid kitchen. Nan and Grandad, who'd just had the shop extended to include a modern kitchen for the commercial baking, then moved to the house next door and let the Rowes have the empty space above the shop. Nan and Grandad then had a kitchen and a modern bathroom added on above the shop kitchen. The Rowes had thought it was wonderful, going from one tiny room to a flat with up-to-date facilities.

With a place of her own now, Mrs Rowe took up her original trade as a dressmaker. They weren't well off, but got by. The new bungalow in Newynn meant Mr Rowe would be able to go out, as he couldn't manage the stairs to and from the flat.

'It'll be good when he can get out and about.' Mrs Rowe smiled. 'Not that we haven't been happy here, ducks, because we have. Coming to live here was a blessing for us.'

'A bungalow with a small garden is perfect.'

'It'll be hard leaving. We'll miss the shop and the neighbours, and your family have been good to us.' She sighed. 'It's been over forty years, you know?'

'Yes.' Susie handed Mrs Rowe her order, 'But Newynn isn't far, and as you've already invited me, I'll be a regular visitor.'

'We're looking forward to it already.'

Mrs Rowe beamed. 'Now what do I owe you for these?'

By the time Susie reached the front of their shop, her thoughts had turned into scary nightmares and despite all intentions to shake them off, vile, ugly threats with the intimation of something far more sinister leached through her.

It was only when Lex made an appearance that she suddenly realised she was daydreaming. It was ironic that she instantly knew Lex was only a dream, while the threats seemed so real.

Her mum looked up and smiled as Susie slipped into the shop. 'How's Mr Rowe?'

Relieved to have other things to think about, Susie shoved the hideous images aside, pushed the vaguely tender materialisation of Lex away and forced a light tone. 'The same.'

'It'll do them both good to live on

ground level,' Gwen said, placing some loaves onto the shelf.

'Yes, but they're going to miss everyone here.'

'They'll make new friends soon enough.' Gwen nodded and gestured to the shelves in the glass fronted counter. 'Before you fill that middle shelf, would you pop a few extra doilies down, please? The custard slices stuck to the shelf yesterday.'

'Of course.' Susie smiled as she went into the kitchen. The modern refrigerated glass counter was Mum's pride and joy, and she couldn't bear seeing it less than pristine.

The immaculate kitchen smelled of freshly baked bread and pastries and yet, although Mum was up baking at five in the morning, there wasn't a speck of flour to be seen. Sometimes Susie wondered whether running a small bakery and grocery shop was worth all the hours her mum put in, yet Gwen never grumbled about the lack of sleep or the long hours she worked.

Dad helped on Friday evenings and Saturday mornings by delivering grocery orders in the van. He was happy working as a furniture maker and restorer, but was immensely proud of Gwen's success.

Occasionally Susie yearned to have a successful business, but what could she do?

'Oh, by the way, Tom came in while you were upstairs,' her mum told her.

Susie's stomach immediately froze as if a glacier of solid ice had erupted in her! Mum seemed rather taken with Tom and had hinted once or twice that now she and Lex were well and truly over, perhaps she ought to consider going out with him.

Susie carried a tray of cream cakes to the counter. 'Oh?' She tried to sound casual.

'I don't know why you're so set against him.'

Susie began arranging several overlapping doilies on the middle shelf.

'I am not dead set, as you put it.'

Yes you are! a voice screamed through her. Taking a deep breath, Susie straightened up.

'Do you think that arrangement of doilies will prevent the cakes sticking?'

Gwen glanced down at the shelf.

'Yes love, thank you.'

Feeling guilty at her outburst about Tom, not to mention the outright lie, she forced her voice to a calm she didn't feel. 'I'm sorry, Mum, but I'm not interested in Tom Prand. I can't force myself to fall in love with him can I?' Every part of her wanted to scream, *I saw Lex yesterday and now I can't stop thinking about him!* All she added though was, 'And you wouldn't want me to lead him on would you?'

'No, of course not.'

Susie's heart soared with relief.

'Mind you,' her mum added, 'he's so polite and always asks after you when he visits.'

'Yes.' Her voice remained steady as she walked into the kitchen. 'He's polite to me when he comes into the shop too.'

'No love, I don't mean just in the shop,' Gwen corrected. 'I mean when he comes in the evenings when you're out flower arranging.' She added as Susie walked back into the shop, 'And he always makes us a lovely cup of tea, too.'

The hairs on the back of Susie's neck rose.

'He comes to our house every Wednesday evening? And makes tea?'

'Most Wednesdays. Didn't you know?'

'You may have told me.' Susie swallowed and told herself firmly to stay calm. 'It must have slipped my mind.'

Gwen smiled wistfully. 'He still has a thing for you, you know, love. He's doing very well now his dad is the manager at the gasworks. He's really settled down.'

Wanting to hide her anxiety Susie squatted down to the shelf again. *I bet he's still in the gang though,* she thought. An undesirable recollection ran through her — she'd hated hanging around with that gang at Patsy's insistence.

The second she thought of Patsy, she also thought of Lex. Again her mind replayed seeing him at the bus stop. She saw his expression, his infinitive gaze, the hurt in his eyes, and his brief but intense contemplation.

Clamping down on her thoughts of Lex, she stood up. 'I think some of those jars need filling, shall I do that?'

The subject of Tom Prand was dropped, but Susie still inwardly seethed.

★   ★   ★

Once the early morning rush was over customers came and went throughout the morning. Often they would stay and chat with each other while she and her mum served other customers; they didn't mind though as the longer they stayed, the more they bought. In fact that was the reason that Nan had expanded from her bakery to general groceries. Some customers would even come in and ask to use the shop telephone to save them walking to the phone box. Gwen didn't mind as it was part of the goodwill, and naturally they paid.

This morning, however, Susie suspected the shop would be buzzing with talk of the previous night's raid and little else.

Her stomach churned. She didn't want it all brought up again, especially as her dad had told her that a *Hetty's* bag was found there. Even though Newynn was nearly two miles away, that bag, with its distinctive logo, meant the raider had been in their shop recently. Either she or Mum could have served them! The thing was though, if that was the case, and the person bought something yesterday, the time narrowed somewhat as Mum always closed the shop promptly at one in the

31

afternoon on Wednesdays.

The shop bell tinkled.

'Morning!'

It was Mrs Shottle from several doors along.

'That was a rum do, wasn't it? Another shop robbed and ransacked!' She paused for effect. 'And a *Hetty's* bag found there.' She made tutting noises. 'To think the robber was in this shop beforehand!'

Susie ignored the icy jolt in her stomach.

'Thankfully it was in Newynn.' She was in such a rush to defend their shop that the words flew from her mouth before she had time to think what she was saying.

'Thankfully?' Mrs Shottle boomed. 'I don't think anyone can be thankful about robberies wherever they took place!'

'No.' Susie wished she could take the words back. 'I meant thankfully it wasn't nearby, but yes, Mrs Shottle, you're quite right. There's nothing thankful about robberies wherever they are.'

'And what about the *Hetty's* bag?'

Goodness, the woman was persistent! Curbing her annoyance, Susie swallowed.

'As you can imagine, Mrs Shottle, Mum's very distressed about that.'

Gwen appeared with a jar of sweets.

'What am I distressed about?'

'The *Hetty's* bag found last night in the raid.'

Gwen stood on tiptoe to put the sweet jar back in place. 'Yes, I've been racking my brains wondering who might have come in here recently that would do such a dreadful thing.' She turned to Mrs Shottle. 'However the constable who came said it could have been in someone's pocket for days or even weeks. As I'm sure you know, they took fingerprints from here too.'

'From what I heard,' Mrs Shottle persisted, 'it was a fresh bag.'

Susie was getting annoyed — this was

ridiculous! She tried to keep her voice composed.

'The bag is not the issue. The issue is that a shop was raided, and the bag found there might or might not have been dropped there by the raider.' Her voice rose as an inner dread seeped through her. 'It might have come from here yesterday morning or last week. We just don't know.' She tried to smile but failed. 'What can I get for you?'

Mrs Shottle scowled. 'Well, there's no need to be like that, young miss. I don't know! Ever since you stopped walking out with that Lex, you've been like a bear with a sore head.' She looked at Gwen. 'Young people these days.'

Gwen beamed. 'Susie's a good girl and I'm lucky to have her here.'

Susie swallowed. She could handle this. She could put Lex from her mind once and for all!

'I'll have my usual Thursday loaf, and I'd like to order a cherry Bakewell for Saturday, please.'

As Susie silently predicted, everyone

coming into the shop that morning wanted to talk about the terrible robbery and the *Hetty's* bag found at the scene. It was because of the bag that the police went from house to house asking if anyone saw anything unusual or suspicious yesterday. Why must every customer mention it, though? By lunchtime, she knew her mum had had enough.

'Why don't you go on in, Mum? I'll shut up the shop then join you for lunch.' She had a thought. 'Why don't you have the afternoon off, for a change? Go into Wynnton to Smites department store and treat yourself to something lovely? I can manage the shop on my own.'

'Why would I want to do that? Besides, Thursday afternoons are their tea and cake afternoons, when all the well-off customers get a private viewing of the latest fashions.'

Susie chuckled. 'Yes, but you could still go. You're always saying you don't get time to shop and they have a sale on at the moment. The well-off don't go to those.'

'I can't just go off. What about you? Wouldn't you like to see what Smites have in their sale?'

'I walk past that store every Wednesday evening, Mum. Besides, you know I enjoy making my own clothes.'

'Even so, you'd benefit from an afternoon of shopping more than I would.' Gwen sighed. 'I know what you're doing, love, and I appreciate it, but I don't need to be wrapped up in cotton wool. Don't think I haven't noticed all the odd looks we've been getting this morning. Just because one of our bags was found at the robbery — ' Gwen drew a determined breath ' — doesn't mean that we're to blame for that in any way.'

'I know Mum, but . . . ' Susie's voice trailed off.

'But nothing. I can withstand a few curious or daggered looks for the time being. So if you bring everything in from the front, I'll check the counter temperature and we can go in for lunch together.'

Susie nodded. Mum's refrigerated counter was the latest boon for shops wanting to display perishable goods rather than having them hidden away in a refrigerated cabinet with the milk and cheeses. The only slight downside was that, due to being opened and shut so many times, the thermostat had to be checked regularly.

'How do *you* feel?' Gwen asked as Susie put the last box of vegetables on the shop floor ready to be put out again when the shop reopened after lunch at two.

Susie stood up and asked, 'What do you mean, how do I feel?'

Gwen hesitated. 'A shadow crossed your face when Mrs Shottle mentioned Lex. You *are* over him, aren't you? After all,' she hurried on before Susie could answer, 'he ditched you without ceremony. I thought you'd forgotten him.'

Susie swallowed. Until last night, she

too had thought she was over Lex. Seeing him at the bus stop brought the longing flooding back, and with the longing came all the wonderful memories of their time together, and he'd hardly been out of her thoughts since.

She was being ridiculous — he was with someone else, someone way more gorgeous and fashionable than she would ever be!

'I was surprised to hear his name mentioned after all this time, that's all,' Susie lied.

'Goodness knows what happened for that family to turn against us in that way.'

It was a subject that had been talked through repeatedly at the time.

'Yes, it's still a mystery,' Susie agreed. And always would be.

★ ★ ★

'Are you sure you want to be in the shop this afternoon, Mum?' Susie had just finished putting the vegetables back

38

outside after lunch. 'I really can manage on my own.'

She hadn't even drawn another breath when the bell tinkled as the door opened. They looked up as the tall dark-haired man, whose shoulders almost filled the doorway, entered. He halted before he reached the glass counter.

'Hello.' His smile was genuine and full of warmth. 'How are you both?'

Susie's stomach lurched as Lex, looking more handsome even than when she last saw him standing at the bus stop the previous night, looked first at Gwen, then at her.

The breath caught in her throat. He hadn't been near the shop in two years! Why was he here now?

'It's been a while,' he said as if he heard her unspoken question. 'As I'm home on leave for two months, so I thought I'd come and see how you all are.'

'Well, talk of the Devil!' Gwen breathed.

'And he appears?' Lex finished with a wry grin.

'Well, we were only talking about you before lunch.' She turned to Susie. 'Weren't we, love?'

Raising a dark quizzing brow for a brief second, Lex chuckled. 'No wonder my ears were burning.'

'I wasn't talking about you!' Susie declared with more determination than she intended. 'You were mentioned by a customer, that's all.' She looked across to where Gwen stood, a damp cloth in her hand, ready to wipe the counter top. 'Isn't that right, Mum?'

'Well, yes,' Gwen replied, then turned to Lex. 'Mrs Shottle mentioned you in passing.'

Susie's stomach flipped slightly. Was that a look of disappointment on his face? Lex raised one brow which made Susie's heart skitter. Inwardly fuming at her own stupidity, she took a breath and looked down at the arrangement of cakes before she lost it altogether and started staring at him like a lovestruck schoolgirl!

They were finished, and besides he was obviously spoken for and therefore out of bounds. Yet, seeing how appealing he was, how glossy his hair looked with the spring sunshine on it, made her heart beat faster and her pain feel almost unbearable. Oh, but just that familiar little habit of raising one brow like that brought all those wonderful sweet memories flooding back!

She didn't need those memories! She didn't need him, and she certainly did not want him to waltz into their shop as if nothing untoward had ever happened between them! Whatever it was that had caused the rift had broken not just her heart, but her spirit too.

Something in her brain flipped. She was determined she could tuck the hurt into the darkest corner of her brain and leave it there forever! All she had to do was detach from, and remain firmly detached from, his charismatic personality.

Looking at her, Lex folded his arms

across his broad chest.

'I wondered,' he began lightly before unfolding his arms and placing one hand on the glass counter. 'If you would consider . . . ' he faltered, which was most unlike him. 'If you would come to the cinema with me. *Gigi* is — '

'I've seen it.' Susie cut in before she could stop herself.

'Oh.' His fingers tapped noiselessly on the glass counter. 'Something else, perhaps?'

Gwen waved in the direction of the street.

'Why don't you both go for a walk? It's a lovely afternoon. You can go for a stroll to the railway bridge and the stream.'

'*Mum!*' Susie muttered beneath her breath.

Lex stopped drumming and held up his hand.

'It's OK, I get it loud and clear,' he said. He turned to Gwen. 'Thanks anyway, Mrs Cotting.'

Gwen darted a look at Susie as he turned to go, a look that said, *It's what you need, Susie!*

Susie's heart thumped and as Lex reached the door, she called out, 'All right.' She schooled her voice to a self-possession she didn't feel. 'A stroll by the stream would be nice.'

As Lex turned to her, Susie's heart skittered again. She saw by his expression that he was pleased and she realised he'd come especially to see her! Mum was right — this was her chance to find out why he dumped her.

With her heart still thumping, Susie went into the kitchen, took off her apron and hung it up next to her coat.

'I'll put my windcheater on,' she called out. 'It can get windy under that bridge.'

Why had she blurted that out? Why hadn't she gone quietly upstairs to get her dolly-mixture blue coat? Now she was being a fool! It was only a walk. Her windcheater would do perfectly well.

3

Once outside they crossed the road from *Hetty's*, and although the maelstrom of thoughts whirling angrily through Susie's head had abated somewhat, she couldn't think of anything to say.

Lex spoke first.

'It's nice now summer is nearly here, isn't it?'

'Yes, it is.'

They lapsed into silence.

As the silence lengthened, Susie wondered if going for a walk with Lex was a good idea after all. How was she supposed to start a conversation with him after all this time? What was she supposed to say? A wisp of annoyance drifted through her — after all, why was it up to her to begin? He had come into the shop to see her, not the other way round. Besides he was the one who had ended their relationship, not her!

Pushing her hands into the windcheater pockets, Susie stayed determinedly quiet.

At last Lex sucked in a breath and said, 'I liked that coat you were wearing.'

'Huh?'

'The pale blue one.'

Was this all he could think of to say after all this time?

'The one you were wearing last night when I saw you on the bus.'

'It's called dolly-mixture blue.'

He dropped his chin in a nod and gave a soft smile. 'Hmm, very apt.'

The look on his face made her insides flutter! Firmly ignoring the silly fluttering, Susie drew a measured breath. 'I bought it in Smites sale. It was the only one left over from one of their private viewings, the ones they have for their well-off customers.'

'That's called 'party plan' in the US.'

Not wanting to appear intrigued Susie frowned up at him.

'Selling things by inviting people to

have a coffee and a chat,' he explained mildly.

Irrespective of his tone, Susie's insides flared. Was he implying their shop wasn't any good?

'That's an expensive way to sell stock. I can't see it catching on here.'

Lex felt a little jolt somewhere deep within him. How had he managed to upset her so much that every word he spoke annoyed her? Suppressing a sigh, he stayed silent as doubt wriggled through him. There was so much he wanted to know yet felt he couldn't ask. He shouldn't have come.

Susie was embarrassed walking along the street like a couple who, having rowed, now had nothing to say to each other. Moreover, it was obvious from the curious looks they were getting from passers-by that that was exactly what they looked like.

Taking a deep breath she gulped. She was going to have to end the excruciating coolness even if it was only for the sake of appearances.

'How are your family?'

He looked down at her in mild surprise.

'Well,' he said. 'Dad has a permanent job at the gasworks, did you know?'

'Yes.'

Len and Beattie were a good few years older than most of the parents with kids of their age. Len, who lost a leg and the use of one eye in WWI, never expected to get married, let alone have children. Not because of his disability, but because of his lack of work prospects. When Beattie came along and fell in love with him, everything changed. They were very poor, though. Before getting the job in the gasworks, the family lived from hand to mouth. If Len managed to get an odd job here and there, the family considered themselves fortunate! It was only Beattie's minuscule wages as a cleaner in the mornings and a cinema usherette in the afternoons and evenings that kept them going.

For as long as Susie could remember,

they were the most impoverished family she knew. A wonderful family for all that, and being Patsy's best friend meant there was nothing they wouldn't do for her. She was considered part of their family just as Patsy was considered part of theirs, especially by Nan when she was alive. Nan adored them both.

'And Patsy — how is she?'

Still looking at her, Lex narrowed his eyes as if surprised by her interest. 'She seems to be doing all right at work. She loved the Post Office sorting office from the moment she started.' He shrugged. 'She's moody at home, though. My parents can't say anything to her without her losing her temper.' He shook his head. 'It's not as if she has anything to be moody about though, now our family are better off than they've ever been. She always has money in her pocket nowadays.'

Susie's stomach roiled at the thought of Patsy's unhappiness. Whatever had gone on between them in recent years, the good years before had to have counted for something.

'Money isn't everything, Lex.'

His heart skipped a beat at the way she said his name just like old times . . . then he remembered.

'I agree, but it helps to have something to fall back on.'

'I know, but having money won't affect how Patsy feels, will it?' She paused recalling how happy-go-lucky Patsy was when they were friends whether she had money or not — and it was usually not. 'She never seemed to envy anyone having things she didn't.'

Lex grinned. 'You and your family made sure she didn't go without too much. Especially that first Christmas after you both became friends.'

He had that misty far-away look in his eyes that Susie knew only too well — and she knew exactly which Christmas he was referring to. Not that she recollected it the way he did. After all, he was nearly seven and she and Patsy were only three. Although her memory of it was vague, Lex had regularly reminded her of it over the years.

'That Christmas,' he continued in the same misty way. 'If I live forever, that Christmas is one I'll never forget.'

Why did he have to bring that up now? Susie whipped her hands from her pockets and clapped them over her ears to block out the sound of his voice. She began to sing, 'La, la, la!' at the top of her voice.

Lex laughed loudly, but persisted. 'Your amazing kindness made it memorable.'

She put her hands down. She knew he was going to tell the story, and she couldn't really walk along the street with her hands over her ears while he talked, could she?

Lex threw back his head and laughed with pure pleasure at the memory. 'Oh, I can still see your little face when Patsy said that Father Christmas wouldn't be coming to our house. There you both were skipping around that old wooden counter, you telling her what Father Christmas was bringing you and her saying she wasn't getting anything.' His laugh of pleasure subsided as he went on. 'That's what it was like in our house. Our parents had to be brutally frank with us both. That year was an especially bad one for them. Not just because of Len's disability either.'

Naturally Susie knew the story. Len Maceul was too disabled to work full time and Mrs Maceul miscarried a baby and wasn't able to work for several months afterwards. And although she couldn't remember Patsy actually telling her that Father Christmas wasn't coming to their house, Susie knew that at that young age, it upset her.

Curbing his gut-wrenching emotion, Lex gave a hoarse chuckle. 'A Meccano set — I thought I'd died and gone to heaven!' He looked down at her. 'I meant to ask. How are Mr and Mrs Rowe?'

Glad he had changed the subject, Susie looked up at him. 'They're moving into their new bungalow on Monday. We're pleased for them but we'll miss them. The place will seem empty without them.'

'I daresay there'll be a few takers for that little flat above such a wonderful shop.'

Aghast, Susie turned on him. 'I don't think my parents are considering renting it out to anyone else. Besides there are all those new places in Newynn. Nobody is going to want a pokey place above a shop when there are those fabulous modern ones for the taking.'

Lex shrugged. 'I hear there's a waiting list for them. I know because some of our neighbours said they're on the list.'

'Mr and Mrs Rowe didn't have to wait long.'

'That's due to Mr Rowe's health.'

Sadness washed over Susie. Mr Rowe was seventy-eight and ill-health had plagued him most of his life. Losing their Alfie hadn't helped either.

That reminded her of their earlier conversation. The Meccano set Lex got for Christmas that year had belonged to Alfie — it had been his tenth birthday present. Mr and Mrs Rowe lovingly kept it for years before parting with it by giving it to Lex, the little boy who had nothing.

Lex genuinely understood the sacrifice Mr and Mrs Rowe had made by parting with it and treasured it all the more. At seven years old and living in poverty, he had to be told there was no such thing as Father Christmas and — unlike Patsy, who did believe — he accepted his lot.

'If it wasn't for you and your concern — '

Susie didn't let him finish. 'Tra, la, la!' she called out, fingers in her ears again. But she couldn't help smiling and, as Lex looked down at her his heart seemed to somersault.

The memory of that year would never leave him and the knowledge that, as young as she was, Susie wanted Patsy to have half of her presents would be engraved on his heart and in his memory forever. It always made him chuckle with delight that, after discovering Patsy wouldn't be getting any presents from Santa, Susie begged her mum and dad to take some of her own presents to Patsy's house, give them to her parents to put in Patsy's room so she would think Father Christmas visited her after all. That simple gesture had had the whole Cotting family, Hetty and Mr and Mrs Rowe in tears as they all rallied round.

Mrs Cotting had bought the doll, and Mrs Rowe made all the clothes a doll could ever need. Hetty was given a second-hand doll's pram that Mr Rowe spruced up so it looked like new and she had made covers for it. Bernie made Patsy a lovely wooden rocking chair and Gwen added a home-made patchwork cushion. Lex and his family were given apples, oranges, dried fruit, and nuts and jams from the shop.

They had all been so close back then, Lex thought. How had it all gone so wrong? Why had the Cottings turned against his family?

His heart lurched as the words of a new song he heard on Radio Luxemburg swept into his mind: *Dream, dream, dream. Whenever I want you, all I have to do is dream, dream, dream.*

His heart raced as the reality hit him — he was still in love with Susie!

He shouldn't have come. He hadn't even known where his feet were taking him until he found himself in their little corner shop.

From the second he'd set eyes on Susie again on the top deck of the bus the previous evening, he knew he wouldn't be able to stay away. Yet for the sake of self-preservation he should have resisted. If it hadn't been for Gwen, she wouldn't even be walking with him now. He was a mad fool!

Forcing his thoughts aside, he changed tack.

'Did you think they'd actually make him go?'

Frowning, Susie stared up at him.

'Into the army to do his National Service?'

Her soft laughter of mild embarrassment as it dawned on her what he meant made his stomach churn. This had to stop!

'It's sad that anyone had to go.'

He shrugged. 'Oh, I don't know, it did me the world of good. Made me realise there was a world out there and I could be a part of something.' He smiled. 'It's given me skills for life.'

Susie's stomach went all fluttery. She should have kept clear of the subject — his going into the RAF to do his National Service five years ago was probably the beginning of the end for them.

Well, not at first, she conceded. At first, they wrote loving letters to each other, and when he was on leave, spent every minute they could together and made such plans for the future.

She fully supported him when he made the decision to stay on and continue training in electronics. After all, if they were going to spend the rest of their lives together, as she believed at the time, she wanted him to be happy for always. It took a while to get used to him being away, but because he was so content it was fine by her and that first year of training he always came home full of enthusiasm for his work.

The fluttering in her stomach intensified. Did he still feel the same way? Did he still love it?

She changed the subject. 'I'm sorry.' She looked up at him sheepishly. 'For tra-la-ing. I was being childish, but . . . Well, there are things I feel awkward talking about.'

'I know. I'm sorry too. But I do think about the past now and then. Don't you?'

How was she supposed to reply to that without sounding hurt, bitter or unhappy? Trying not to heave a heavy sigh, she forced her lips to smile and swallowed. 'Sometimes.' She hoped she sounded matter-of-fact.

They reached the road leading to the railway arch. Susie loved it here at this time of year when the embankment was alive with spring wild flowers. Goodness knows how they flourished year after year with all that smoke from the trains above though. 'Look at the baby rabbits!'

Lex, well aware that the subject had been changed because either there were things she didn't want to discuss or because she didn't know what he was about to say, followed her gaze.

'With all those burrows under that railway bank, I'm surprised the whole thing doesn't collapse.'

'Lex!'

Hearing her use his name like that again had a double-whammy effect on him. On the one hand he was elated that it rolled so easily from her tongue. On the other hand, it brought all the yearning and all the memories of what was and might-have-been that it dampened his spirits.

'Sorry,' he murmured with genuine remorse.

Susie smiled. Walking with him seemed so natural. It was as though they'd never been apart. Their old rapport was slowly returning and she had the deep longing to take hold of his hand. Thrusting her hands firmly back into her pockets, she remained doggedly determined to keep her distance, emotionally as well as physically.

The Victorian railway bridge arching over the road at the end of Willbob Street signalled the end of the developed area of the west of Oldwynn. Beyond the bridge were footpaths leading to craggy countryside.

The stream Susie's mum mentioned was once a fast flowing river. Eons ago, when the canal was built however, pipes leading from it were also constructed to siphon some of the river water into the canal. Now all that remained was often not much more than a narrow trickle. It had a lovely gently sloping bank though, so it was a popular family picnic area because it was clean and shallow enough for children to paddle in.

A sudden panic whipped through Susie. It wasn't such a safe place to be at night any more, though! She'd once been here with Patsy and the gang, and the guys had gone off into a huddle. Their conversation, although muted, was full of snorts of derision, chortling and guffaws of self-satisfaction. She'd caught one or two phrases such as 'dire consequences' and 'all squealers suffer'. There was considerable back slapping and glee as if something was being sorted out. Then they formed a circle, jointly shook hands, and Susie was sure they took some kind of oath. It chilled her then, and it still chilled her now.

Compelling her thoughts into a padlocked part of her brain, she swiftly replaced them. She, Lex and Patsy often came on summer evenings or lazy Sundays and she always loved coming here. Even when the trains whistled by, the place was still magical.

Susie was so wrapped up in the memories that by the time they reached the water, she realised they'd lapsed into total silence again.

Suddenly they both spoke at once . . .

'Do — ?'

'Isn't it — ?'

They both chuckled.

Lex waved his hand. 'You go on.'

Feeling self-conscious, Susie shook her head.

'No, you first.'

He bowed ever so slightly. 'Ladies first.'

It seemed such a silly question now, and he may think she was only trying to make conversation rather than show a real interest. Yet — and her mind whirred and her heart thumped with the realisation — she *was* interested!

'Do you still love the work you're doing in the RAF?' she asked.

He blinked in amiable surprise. 'Yes, but . . . ' He hesitated. 'Well, this two-month-long leave will give me time to decide if I want to sign up for another two or five years, or branch out into a commercial work environment.'

They were just starting to step onto the narrow little path on the bank above the stream. Although Susie smiled, her stomach jolted. Not just because she was here with him, but also because of his reply.

'Don't get me wrong Susie, life in the services is rewarding, but . . . ' He sighed. 'Maybe now's the time to consider my options, that's all.' He drew another breath. 'Have you been abroad?'

Suddenly overcome by an indefinable annoyance, Susie glared up at him and snapped, 'You know I haven't!'

A little shocked by her lone, Lex gathered his thoughts before replying steadily, 'I don't necessarily know that, Susie.'

Susie inwardly winced. Why had she rounded on him like that?

'For all I know, you could have spent

your holidays sunning yourself in Majorca.'

Susie's insides jumped at the direct reference to their break-up.

Lex could have bitten his tongue out! While longing for an explanation about what had gone wrong, he didn't want conflict either.

'Well, I haven't. You on the other hand, have been all over the world.'

He tensed slightly, but kept his tone neutral.

'Not quite, Susie. But did you know I was in Suez for a while?'

Susie's insides knotted. Lex in danger? She felt nauseous and dizzy! 'No, I didn't.'

She must be sensible — she had no right to know about his life and asking him what he'd been doing and where he'd been stationed would be prying. They were no longer a couple. Yet her heart sang when she realised how well they were getting along — it was almost like old times.

'It was tough on my folks,' Lex went

on and shrugged. 'But as you can see I'm in one piece.'

Susie knew he really meant that he wasn't injured like his dad had been during WWI. It must have been absolutely unbearable for them knowing Lex was caught up in the Suez crisis!

How would she feel if anything happened to him? It didn't bear thinking about.

No, she was being melodramatic — nothing was going to happen to Lex. Conscription was different from general wartime call-up wasn't it? Besides, conscription was ending soon and, as Lex just said, he could please himself whether he stayed in the RAF or if, after his initial two years — like so many other young men — he chose to stay on to continue training.

She hoped he couldn't hear her thumping heart as a result of all these conflicting thoughts she was having.

'It's good that you came home safe and sound.' She aimed for casual yet thoughtful but her words came out on a sigh so instead she sounded blissfully relieved — which she was!

If he noticed, he never let on.

'Yes, and I think Mum and Dad are glad that if I stay in the RAF I'll be at North Coates in Lincolnshire for the next two years.'

4

Susie was determined that she must not think of Lex working so close to home, yet her treacherous heart skipped a beat. North Coates was less than half an hour away on the train.

'If you left, would you miss going abroad?' she asked him, trying to sound calm and casual.

'Maybe, but even in a commercial environment I might still be travelling. If I do sign up for two more years though, I'll be much better qualified and there'll be even more opportunities for me.'

Her stomach began twirling with joyfully sparkling minuscule diamond-clad dancers. Quashing it all and feeling silly, she said, 'You always wanted to go into the Air Force, didn't you?' Her foolish heart swelled with pride as a memory rushed straight from her brain and out of her mouth. 'There were times when you talked of nothing else.'

'I must have been a pain,' he said ruefully.

Oh, she must start behaving like an adult, not a lovelorn ex who couldn't bear to let her sweetheart go! Her silly heart and dancing insides had to be ignored — or quashed once and for all! The past was the past, and whatever went wrong between them had to be put aside for the sake of any future friendship — at least she hoped they could move on and become friends.

She purposely kept her tone light as she said, 'No, you weren't. You just wanted to fight for your country. All boys did then, didn't they?'

His blue eyes twinkled and one dark brow quirked. 'You knew what all boys wanted to be when they grew up?'

Without thinking she turned and playfully nudged him with her shoulder. 'Oh, you know what I mean.'

The familiarity of the gesture seared through Lex and his heart leaped as overwhelming happiness wheeled through him. As he looked down at her upturned face he had an irresistible urge to kiss her!

He mustn't! Whatever had happened to cause her to ditch him as she had was still there, and while kissing her now might make him feel good for a while, there would still be that stumbling block obstructing his path. The Tom Prand stumbling block.

The painful memory of seeing Prand's arm round Susie's shoulders rushed back before he could prevent it.

They were all in the park, Susie and Patsy and the shady gang they'd started to go around with. He was on weekend leave and had gone to meet Susie and ask why he hadn't received a letter from her recently.

He was a fool — he should never have gone to the shop to see her now! What was he thinking?

Turning rapidly away from her he noticed something in the stream and changed the subject.

'Just look at those tadpoles.'

Susie had the absurd feeling that Lex wanted to kiss her and something within her had welled up with the sheer joy and expectation of it, but then his expression changed suddenly and that joy crashed round her feet.

Oh, why had she agreed to go on this walk? She shouldn't have come! This wasn't just bringing back memories, it was giving her false hope.

Yet, the memory of how she Patsy and Lex came to the stream to see the frogspawn turning into tadpoles and then tiny frogs came reeling back. It seemed so childish now, but had been so much fun back then.

She had to get a grip! Shoving her thoughts aside, she squatted beside Lex to get a better look and, despite her inner turmoil, realised there was still something uniquely uplifting about watching new life beginning.

'Most of them will be picked off by greedy predators before June.'

Right on cue — it was what he had

always said back then, too!

Trailing her fingers through the surface of the water beside his, she nodded sadly. 'Yes.'

Without warning, their hands touched and the shockwave was as instant as it was unexpected. Snatching her trembling hand from the water she stood up. 'I ought to be getting back.'

He sighed and she felt the atmosphere change completely. He was standing quite still now, staring languidly across the little stream as if concentrating on the shrub-lined bank beyond.

'What went wrong, Susie?'

He spoke so softly, she wondered if she imagined it. Suddenly her world stood still. What did he mean, what went wrong? *She* was the one who should be asking him that!

'I don't know. You tell me, Lex.'

He turned to gaze directly down at her.

'I was hoping you'd tell me.'

Lex's heart was pounding so hard, he feared she could hear it. Her expression was of bewildered hurt — the same expression he saw when she was on the bus.

'I'm sorry,' he muttered, 'I didn't mean it to come out like that. It's just that . . . ' He paused as a blistering pain engulfed him. An inner voice thundered at him to stop now, but he couldn't. He had to know. 'Well, it's just that it ended so abruptly, and I didn't know why.'

Susie drew back in complete shock. 'What do you mean? Of course you knew why!'

'So it was Tom Prand then?'

Susie felt as though she'd been slapped in the face and the shock nearly made her lose her balance as she stepped back.

'Tom Prand?' she echoed. 'I wouldn't touch him with a barge pole!'

Wheeling away from Lex before she lost her footing down the bank, Susie attempted to swallow her anger. She would not rise to whatever bait Lex was throwing out! Tom Prand? Her stomach roiled and her head began to swim.

She didn't know how it happened, but the next moment Lex had his arms tightly round her, holding her up.

'Hey! I thought you were about to faint, there!'

'My legs just gave way,' she managed to whisper through a fuzzy haze. She opened her eyes but, while enjoying his familiar masculine scent, didn't look up. It felt as though they'd never been apart.

'Are you OK now?' he asked, deeply concerned.

Still disorientated but enjoying the blissful sensation of being so close to him Susie raised her chin to look at him. 'I think so.'

Suddenly he longed to taste the sweetness of her soft lips, yearned to hold her and never let go of her again!

Instead, he released her with measured reluctance. 'Let me know if you feel dizzy again.'

Steadying herself and feeling somewhat awkward by whatever it was that just happened, Susie nodded. 'Yes, I'm all right now.'

Slowly compelling his arms back to his sides, Lex let her edge away from him.

'I think I must have turned too quickly and caused all the blood to rush from my head,' she said. The truth was, she didn't know why she had such a turn and couldn't even recall what they were talking about immediately beforehand. 'I'd better be getting back to the shop.'

Lex nodded, unnerved, and swallowed hard. Oh, but it was a joy to have her in his arms again!

Her colour hadn't returned yet so he offered his arm. 'I think you should put your arm through mine,' he said quietly.

'Thank you, Lex.'

Susie must have still been feeling dazed when they reached the railway bridge otherwise she would never have mentioned it. 'This is where that gang

Patsy goes around with hangs out now.'

Oh no! Why had that popped out of her mouth? Then to make things worse, another totally unwanted thought came into her head.

Suddenly another image rushed into her mind — with a voice that was harsh and menacing as it growled, 'You're in it with us. Understand? There's no going back. Traitors get punished.'

A strange feeling came over Susie as she tried to shake the image away. Why did these ridiculous visions come into her head, anyway? She quickened her pace.

Lex didn't want to hear about Susie with Prand or the gang, wanted to be anywhere but here — yet he also wanted to be with Susie, wanted more than anything else in the World to taste the sweetness of her lips. But now she was hurrying as if she couldn't bear his company any longer.

'I hope you don't go out alone at night,' he suddenly blurted out. What right had he to demand that? Besides, he'd seen her out alone last night — but maybe she wasn't alone . . . was there someone new since Prand?

Taken aback by his remark, Susie blurted without thinking, 'Only to and from Wynnton on Wednesday nights.'

'You don't go to dancing in Oldwynn village hall any more?'

Susie's stomach knotted. The gang still went there. 'No.'

'You loved dancing.' She was still pale and Lex wasn't sure she was over her initial upset. 'You never go jiving now?'

The memory of jiving with Patsy and what was then a group of friends to the music of Bill Hayley and his Comets slowed her down as a brief shaft of grief shot through her.

Those days had gone, but she couldn't help remembering flipping back her strawberry blonde ponytail that was now a more grown-up tied-back demi-wave. Her dancing pumps along with layers of net underskirts now cluttered her wardrobe and hadn't seen the light of day for years.

All that was in the past now — Patsy had made it abundantly clear that the gang despised her.

'I have other interests now.'

Lex's insides jolted. What other things — did she mean a boyfriend? Prand came instantly to mind, but after her horrified reaction just prior to her near faint, he knew better than to ask.

'Like going to the cinema to see *Gigi*?' He cleared his throat awkwardly. 'I'm sorry, that just came out. It's just that when you said you'd seen it, I presumed it was last night when I saw you on the bus.'

Susie didn't want to elaborate, yet for some reason she wanted him to know she that didn't have a boyfriend. 'I go to an evening class.'

He was intrigued. 'What kind of class?'

Susie couldn't tell him what sort of a class it was but neither did she want to lie either.

'Just a class.'

Lex frowned. What was it she didn't want him to know — and why?

'I know — it must be sewing. You always loved sewing and wanted to use the Rowes' flat to start your own sewing business. Now you could.'

'I hadn't thought of that! What a good idea!'

Intrigued, but not wanting to pester her, Lex curbed his curiosity and remained silent, but going through in his mind all the things she might be studying. Then he had a sudden unwelcome thought — was there someone she was keen on at the evening class? He hoped not!

Pushing the thoughts aside, he drew a relaxed breath. 'I'd like to do this again,' he smiled. 'What about you?'

Susie's stomach somersaulted! Had Lex just asked her out? No, of course not — he was just being friendly. After all, he had a girlfriend, didn't he? A gorgeous, smart, up-to-the-minute, exquisitely groomed girlfriend. A girlfriend who was obviously utterly besotted with him — and what girl would not be besotted with Lex Maceul?

Her spirits plummeted.

Forcing her voice into a semblance of serenity she didn't feel, Susie beamed up at him.

'Yes, why not?' she said.

Lex's heart skipped a beat, but then something inside him jolted as a thread of guilt ran through him. Even as just friends, in spite of her prickliness, he'd enjoyed Susie's company for this brief half-hour far more than all the dates he'd had with Gloria put together. It was as if he'd snatched a brief but longed for moment of happiness he didn't deserve.

'In that case how about tomorrow lunchtime? I'll bring a picnic lunch.'

Susie's heart skipped. Should she really be going for picnics and walks with another girl's boyfriend?

'I'll do the sandwiches, you can buy a couple of Mum's cakes,' she said.

* * *

Gwen looked up and smiled as Susie and Lex came back into the shop.

'Hello. Have you two had a pleasant walk?'

Lex smiled. 'It was great, wasn't it, Susie?'

Feeling a sudden rush of warmth and an unexpected fluttering of delight, all Susie could do was nod in agreement.

'Good,' Gwen said with genuine pleasure. 'Goodness,' she continued in a flurry as if not wanting to dwell on the subject, 'folk are asking if there's going to be a farewell do for the Rowes.'

'I think we should,' Susie said. 'Mention it to Mrs Shottle and she'll have it sorted before you can say egg whisk!'

Gwen laughed but then immediately sighed. 'I'm thrilled for them naturally, but I'll miss them.'

'You might be able to re-let the flat when they've gone,' Lex said.

Susie scowled at him. How could he suggest that after she had made it clear that her parents had no intention of getting another tenant?

'Lex! Mum and Dad won't consider any such thing!' She turned to her mum. 'Would you?'

Surprised at Susie's outburst, Gwen blinked.

'Well, I can't say we've thought of it let alone discussed it, but on reflection it would be going to waste if we don't consider all our options.'

'Mum!' Susie gasped.

'I know how you feel, love. The Rowes have been here over forty years and like you I couldn't imagine anyone else being there. But we have enough space and I daresay there'll be someone out there in need of a roof over their head.'

'Nobody will want a tiny flat like when there are all those new places being built at Newynn.'

Lex cleared his throat and cut in. 'But there's a long waiting list.'

Why was Lex so keen for them to have new tenants in their flat? It had nothing to do with him!

'What's it to you?' Susie demanded.

Lex threw up his hands. 'Whoa, it's just a suggestion, that's all. I didn't mean to upset you.'

'I'm sure Lex means well, Susie,' Gwen soothed. 'While letting the flat isn't something we've thought about, perhaps we should. There may be someone in need of a cosy little place.'

'Or a business venture, perhaps?' Lex said, giving Susie a wink.

Cross at Lex for bringing it up, as well as alarmed at the thought of a stranger in such close proximity, Susie swallowed hard. Business venture? Now he was trying to butter her up!

'I need to be getting back to work Lex. Unlike some, I don't have two months' leave!'

With that, she zipped behind the counter, whisked her apron from the hook on the door and flounced off into the shop kitchen. She didn't go back into the shop until at least ten minutes after hearing the doorbell go.

5

Apart from chatting to their customers, Susie and her mum spent the rest of the afternoon in less than companionable silence. It was nearly closing up time before Susie felt she could speak without getting upset.

'Do you want me to re-price the last two loaves and those three cream horns now?'

The shop was usually quiet after half-past four, then sometimes at about twenty past five, a flurry of customers wanting to catch the shop before it closed came scurrying in. If there were a couple of perishables left, Gwen reduced the prices a bit, and Susie suspected some waited until the last moment just to get cheaper goods.

Gwen checked the clock. 'Give it another five minutes, love.'

That familiar endearment soothed

Susie's frayed nerves. 'I'll start bringing the vegetable shelves in from outside, then,' she offered.

Once outside on the pavement in front of the shop, the fresh cool afternoon air reminded her of her walk with Lex, something she resolutely refused to dwell on since flouncing off earlier. Now though, she doubted she would see him again. In spite of their plans for lunch tomorrow it was unlikely he'd be back.

Her spirits fell. Why had he come, anyway? After two years, why had he waltzed into the shop — and then had the gall to ask *her* what had gone wrong? A strange feeling swept through her as she recalled what Lex said about Patsy — that she was over the moon when she'd started at the sorting office.

'All those letters from all over the world, and I'm part of that. I'll never tire of it,' he had told her Patsy said.

Patsy had been happy-go-lucky in those days. She was never moody, always saw the positive side of things.

As far as Susie recalled, Patsy adored her parents and was considerate and caring towards them. She was over the moon when Len had got a permanent job at the new gasworks too and, as Lex pointed out, the whole family were financially better off than they had ever been.

As for losing her temper, the first time Susie experienced that was at the dreadful falling-out after she'd told Patsy she wasn't going to go around with the gang any more. It was then that Patsy said the Maceul family didn't want anything more to do the Cotting family.

Brushing the memories away, Susie bent down to pick up a box of tomatoes and a slight movement from the corner opposite the shop caught her eye. Swinging round, she frowned. The corner was deserted. Had she imagined it? Brushing off the peculiar chill slithering down her spine, she picked up the tomatoes and stepped over to the shop door. It was then she caught sight of a dishevelled young man skulking along the street. His hair was tousled, he was thin, and his clothes looked shabby.

Susie took the box of tomatoes into the kitchen larder. 'There's a rumpled young guy I don't recognise coming towards the shop,' she said.

Gwen looked up from her wiping. 'I've heard that a couple with a baby and an older son moved into the other side of Oldwynn. The boy's a bit light-fingered, so they say, and is banned from several of the local shops. Apparently his father had to return some of the pilfered items.'

'Perhaps the family are hard-up.'

'Maybe, but there's poor folk who wouldn't think thieving is the answer. I've heard his father is pretty hard on him.' She sighed. 'But it's just gossip, so keep an eye out just in case.'

As she went to fetch another box, Susie noticed the young man had stopped to tie a frayed shoelace. Was he planning to steal something from outside their shop, and just loitering until she went back inside?

Susie stooped to pick up another tray. Suddenly he was beside her.

'Here, let me help.'

Looking up, Susie was immediately struck by how much shabbier he looked close up.

Her thoughts involuntarily turned to Lex and their conversation regarding how little money his parents had then and how much better things were now. Maybe things would be the same for this young man soon? There was a kindness in his expression and tone that made her heart go out to him.

'Thanks,' she gave him a genuine smile, 'but I'm used to it.' Seeing his obvious disappointment she relented. 'That box of potatoes need to be taken in, though.'

The smile that sprang to his lips made her heart sing and her acceptance of help worthwhile.

Gwen looked up as they both went into the shop carrying a box each. 'You have help, I see.'

'That's right, missus.' The young man copied Susie by carefully placing the box of potatoes to one side of the shop floor under a window. As he stood up again, he tugged at a clump of messy brown hair on his forehead. It was an act of courtesy Susie hadn't seen for a long time.

'Should I bring the rest in, missus?' he asked.

To Susie's surprise her mum smiled. 'That would be most kind of you, young man.'

'Do you think that's the boy from that family we were just talking about?' Susie whispered once he was outside.

'I haven't seen him around before, so I think it must be.' Gwen shrugged. 'But he doesn't look the sort to take a sweet that's been dropped on the pavement, let alone steal from shops.'

'Poor mite looks half-starved and although I feel bad for saying it, his clothes need mending.'

'Shhh, he's coming back. Look at his feet.'

As the boy came through with another box of vegetables, Susie looked at his feet. His bare toes were sticking out from shoes with gaping holes in them!

'That's very kind of you,' Susie said to the boy as she glanced at her mum and then at the two loaves on the counter. Her mum nodded. 'Could you use those two loaves of bread?'

The boy raked a hand through his hair. 'I don't have any money with me, missus.'

Gwen, who was already wrapping the loaves in brown paper smiled. 'On the house,' she said.

'For bringing in the boxes,' Susie added.

'I'd best bring in the rest then,' he added rather seriously.

Watching two women hurrying to get to the shop before each other, Susie pointed to the cream cakes. 'What about those?'

Gwen eyed the two women outside vying for prime position and grinned. 'Yes, of course.' She picked up a *Hetty's* bag, bent to the cabinet again, and popped the three cakes into it. By the time the two women came into the shop, there were no loaves or cream cakes on view.

'Too late,' one observed, disappointed.

'Shame,' replied the other.

Gwen shook her head. 'It's been a busy day. Is there anything else I can get you?'

★　★　★

By the time all the boxes were in the shop, the two women had gone and by that time, Gwen had put one or two other goodies in a brown *Hetty's* carrier bag ready for the boy to take with him.

After telling them he hadn't expected anything and thanking them profusely, he hesitated.

'I've just come back from Newynn. I

was looking for work there.'

'What sort of work?' Gwen asked.

He shrugged. 'Anything really.'

'What would you do if you had the choice?'

'I wanted to go into the RAF for my National Service, get training for something.'

Susie's heart flipped. She must stop thinking of Lex at every turn!

'But my dad wouldn't hear of it.' The boy sighed. 'There are lots new shops going up so I was hoping to get some labouring work — you know, shop fitting. But there's nothing.'

Susie tried not to look at him with too much sympathy. He looked too scrawny to hoist large fittings around. 'What about an apprenticeship?'

He shrugged. 'My dad said there's not enough money in it.'

'But there would be eventually.'

'That's what Mam told him, but he said that by that time I'd be married and they would have made the sacrifices but get none of the benefit.

Besides,' he added, 'I'm too old to apply now.'

What a shame that such an eager young man was being prevented from bettering himself just because a parent wasn't prepared to make a small sacrifice.

'There's the gasworks,' Gwen suggested.

'Dad works there and told me there's nothing going. He's well in with the gaffer, so he knows.'

Susie's stomach churned. 'Is that Tom Prand's stepdad?' The boy nodded. 'I know it isn't much, but if you help bring the boxes in every day until you find something permanent you can have the odds and ends of the leftover perishables.'

The boy's face lit up. 'Mam would be fine with that, but . . . ' His face fell. 'Dad wouldn't like it.'

'Occasionally, then?'

He nodded. 'Yes, if I'm not working.'

★   ★   ★

After giving everything the once-over and locking up, Susie and Gwen left the shop through the kitchen back door, then through the dividing fence gate into their own back yard.

Susie was relieved that in the winter they didn't have to walk round into the alley in the dark. The gate her dad put in had made things much easier. It was better for the Rowes too, because that meant the original stairway leading to the front door on the street was just theirs.

'Dad says he's thinking of having a security light put up on our gate so that a light comes on when anyone comes past.'

'Yes, but it might be a nuisance for the neighbours having a light go on and off at the slightest movement.'

Her mum had a point, and a thread of unease coiled through Susie. 'I like the idea of a security light,' she persisted. 'It may deter — ' She was about to say raiders, but just managed to stop herself just in time and instead said, 'intruders.'

Opening their kitchen door, Gwen pivoted round to face her daughter. 'What intruders?'

Susie wished she could take the words back.

'Would-be intruders,' she quickly amended.

'I'm sure our shop isn't important enough to attract those awful raiders, love,' Gwen reassured. her. 'Besides, the shops being targeted don't have the owners living next door, and aren't on a corner, so I think we're safe.'

She suddenly changed the conversation. 'Are you looking forward to seeing Lex again?'

Susie's stomach flipped at both the mention of his name and the fact that she doubted he planned to come back.

'I don't think he'll be back after the way I stomped off, do you?'

Her mum gave her a curious look. 'He said he'd be back tomorrow lunchtime, said you were making sandwiches and he'd buy the cakes.'

Banishing all thoughts of would-be intruders or raiders, Susie's spirits suddenly soared and she realised she was humming Perry Como's latest hit, *Magic Moments*.

★　★　★

Susie was completely unable to move.

'You and your family will pay, Susie Cotting.'

The voice was always the same — male, determined and menacing.

'Giving me the cold shoulder, turning me down, then walking off! That's going to have consequences and soon you'll understand what those consequences are. I have ways of influencing people.'

The voice always ended with a snarl. Susie wanted to know who was so threatening and why. Yet she felt powerless. Why couldn't she escape these horrible dreams? Sometimes she was unable to move because he barred her way. Sometimes he was so close she could smell him and she woke up retching, but she managed to tell herself it wasn't real.

This time, though, there was something else that happened in the dream. Suddenly, the shop was being rifled and the till being raided and the security light didn't work! The security light! Oh no, due to Mum's misgivings Dad hadn't fitted it! It was too dark and nobody else knew what was happening because they were all in bed!

Susie was the only one who knew — only she could see the stuff all over the floor and the counter! Oh no, her mum's counter being smashed, everything destroyed! She tried to get out of bed but her legs refused to move. She tried to shout for help, but no sound came out.

Then just as suddenly as it came, the dream vanished, she was able to move, and she sat up in bed thankful it was over. Shaking but relieved, she waited for a few breathless moments before slipping out of bed and going to the window. Her bedroom faced the street, and as she peered through the curtains she saw the last strands of darkness threading westward.

★ ★ ★

Bernie was finishing off his breakfast as Susie walked into the kitchen.

'Morning love, did you sleep well?'

Supressing an icy shiver, Susie managed to smile. 'Yes, although I was awake before my alarm went off.' She didn't add, *because I had a vile dream and was glad to be awake!*

His expression became serious. 'I hear you're seeing Lex again today.'

Susie's spine shimmied at the same time as her insides danced with euphoric diamond-clad ballerinas. But no — she mustn't read too much into their outing! Lex had a girlfriend, she reminded herself.

'It's just a picnic, Dad.'

'Susie — ' he began, but before he

could finish, Gwen came through with the post.

'Two bills, Bernie,' she announced, putting them on the small breakfast table in front of him. 'And a local handwritten one.'

Ignoring the bills, Bernie opened the hand written letter, reading it in silence, and frowned. He refolded the letter, put it back into the envelope and thrust it into a back trouser pocket. 'The gossip chariot's been out for a blather jaunt!'

'Who's it from?' Gwen asked.

'We'll discuss it tonight.'

'You can at least tell us who sent it,' Gwen huffed, 'or Susie and I will be worrying all day.'

Pushing his chair back, Bernie stood up. 'That was a wonderful breakfast, as usual, love. I don't know how you do it after baking for the shop.' He leaned over and kissed Gwen's cheek. 'I'll be back at my usual Friday time for the deliveries.'

'I'll be ready,' Susie said.

Some customers liked buying their

groceries once a week and having them delivered on Friday evenings or Saturday mornings. Susie always went with him on Fridays and they went to the fish and chip shop for their Friday family supper.

'Unless anything else comes up?' Bernie's eyebrows rose.

Susie knew exactly what he was hinting at. 'No Dad, I can assure you it won't.'

'Oh, Mum,' Susie sighed after he left. 'Have you been putting ideas into his head about Lex?'

'Well I mentioned you went out for a walk with him and that you're going on a picnic today.' She narrowed her gaze. 'It's not a secret, is it?'

'Of course not, but I don't want anyone misinterpreting the situation. He has a girlfriend.'

Gwen puffed out a breath. 'Oh, I didn't realise that. Well, at least he was honest with you, love.'

An inexplicable pain shot through Susie. 'I saw them together at the bus stop on Wednesday.'

Gwen's brow furrowed. 'Maybe she's just a friend?' she suggested.

Susie nearly scoffed, but tempered her tone to one of composure. 'I doubt it, judging from the dreamy look in her eyes.'

Mum raised a quizzical brow. 'So you were close enough to see that, were you?'

'I was on the top deck of the bus at the time. But close enough to see that she's gorgeous.'

Gwen drew back a little. 'Not more gorgeous than my beautiful Susie!'

Deciding not to take that remark any further Susie poured herself a cup of tea.

★　★　★

To Susie's relief, the shop hadn't been ransacked, the refrigerated counter was intact, the morning went by as usual, and to Susie's relief nobody mentioned anything about the Wednesday night raid and the *Hetty's* bag.

During the morning she took some time out to make cheese and pickle sandwiches that she put in a wicker basket with two bottles of ginger-beer and a bottle opener before placing it all in the larder so it would still be fresh at lunchtime.

Throughout the morning she dithered about whether to go and change into something a little less workday. On the one hand she didn't want to look on their outing as a romantic date and risk scaring him off by going over the top. Then again, she didn't want to appear as if she didn't care about it either.

She had some fashionable clothes in her wardrobe, but what she had a real yen to wear was her new turquoise polka-dot Easter dress. Would it be too dressy? Then she had another thought. Would they go to the stream again or would he suggest somewhere else? She was in such a quandary! Should she even bother to change into something else? After all, she hadn't changed from her work clothes yesterday.

There again, she didn't know he was going to turn up yesterday did she? And so it went on . . .

Half an hour before lunchtime she still hadn't made a decision! With only ten minutes to spare, Susie finally made a decision.

'I don't want to go out in my work clothes, do you mind if I go upstairs to change?' she asked.

Gwen grinned, 'I wondered when you were going to go and get ready.'

When Susie finally reappeared, Gwen smiled broadly. 'You look lovely,' she said.

Not wanting to appear over-keen, Susie shrugged with a nonchalance she didn't feel — she was buzzing with excitement. She went to get the lunch basket, thinking she would have worn the pink pedal-pushers and angora sweater even if there had been a blizzard outside!

6

Lex arrived looking so handsome that Susie's heart skittered and those diamond-clad ballerinas began dancing in her stomach again! It was obvious he had made an effort to look his best and her spirits soared that he had.

The white shirt he wore under his fashionable black and grey Argyle sweater was crisply pressed, his narrow grey trousers sharply creased, and his shoes were freshly polished. His glimmering dark hair was in as much of a quiff at the front as the short RAF length would allow — and was that a citrus-wood aftershave wafting towards her?

Lex's heart leapt the moment he saw her, she looked so fabulous. Her strawberry blonde hair was elegantly backcombed and clipped at the back with the length flowing to just above her shoulders. Her pink fluffy sweater was adorable and matched her fashionable pedal pushers.

'Hi, Lex.' Not wanting to show how delighted she was to see him or reveal the effect he was having on her, Susie immediately held up the basket. 'It's ready, except for the cakes.'

She wanted to run back into the kitchen to hide her turbulent emotions and try to control the maelstrom of feelings swirling through her! She had to get a grip — this wasn't a date! They were just two friends having lunch together.

Taking a deep breath as the memory of the speed and the way in which he had ditched her came back, she firmly quashed all the idiotic tumult within her.

'Perfect,' he murmured. 'I ordered cakes and two nectarines yesterday.'

The quirk of his brow sent her spirits soaring again, but determined to remain outwardly calm she braved herself for his drop-dead gorgeous smile and nodded. Nectarines were one of her favourites. Had Lex remembered or had her mum reminded him?

She had to be on her guard — more than that, she needed to wrap herself in an invisible amour of cool indifference! She had to fortify herself against Lex's charisma or his genuinely kind persona would be her undoing all over again if she didn't watch out!

Now wishing she hadn't made such an effort, Susie nodded at her mum wrapping the cakes. 'They can go in the basket.'

Lex directed his dazzling smile at Susie, then turned to Gwen. 'Here, let me.'

Susie's knees went weak! How could this happen in such a short space of time? How could she have gone from doggedly and repeatedly ousting him from her mind throughout the last two years to feeling lovestruck within days? For the sake of her sanity she had to keep things in perspective. They were only friends.

'Susie?'

The way he said her name made her stomach flip. It brought back the memory of how close they once were. She steeled herself to remain casual as she said, 'Yes, I'm ready.'

Wondering why she'd allowed her foolish heart to skitter and her silly knees to go weak, Susie silently followed him out of the shop.

'Shall we go to the stream again?' Lex asked.

'I don't mind, whatever you think.'

'It's what I had in mind when arranging it yesterday.' He paused. 'But how about we walk along the street today?'

Susie suddenly felt panicked — what would they talk about? Had he told Patsy and his parents about them meeting up? If he had, what did they think about it? After all, Patsy had made it clear that his family wanted nothing more to do with their family, hadn't she?

'What did your parents and Patsy say

when you told them you came to the shop yesterday?'

'I didn't tell Patsy. She was up in her room all evening. Goodness knows what's got into her! Except for when Gloria was here she's hardly spoken two words to me since I came home.'

Gloria? Susie should have known such a beautiful girl would have a name to match! 'Gloria being the girl I saw you with at the bus stop?'

Although it wasn't visible, she felt him tense. Why had she been so insensitive as to ask the obvious? Now he would think she was jealous!

'I'm sorry, Susie, I should have told you about Gloria yesterday.' He swallowed hard. 'But I guess the conversation never came up.'

Susie forced a smile. 'You don't have to tell me anything, Lex. What you do and when you do it is your own affair.'

Somewhat hurt, he came to an immediate standstill and stared down at her.

'Gloria and I are not having an affair!'

Oh, why had she used the word affair? Now she'd wounded him!

'I didn't mean it like that,' she replied hastily. 'I meant that what you do is your own business.'

Lifting his head and fixing his gaze in the distance, he drew a breath. 'I suppose it is.'

'Patsy and your parents like her?'

He looked down at her again. 'I suppose so. You know what my parents are like. They never have a bad word to say about anyone.'

Susie's stomach turned over. It was true the Meceuls were never unkind about anyone. So why had they turned their backs on her family?

'Patsy's effort surprised us, considering the way she is with everyone else.'

'Have your parents asked her what's wrong?'

Lex shrugged. 'Yes, but she just clams up and if they keep asking, she tells them not to interfere in her life and flies off in a huff to her room. If either of them confronts her while she's going off on one she shouts that they have no idea what it's like to be her.'

'Do you think there's something going on in her life that's worrying her?'

'Beats me, I just wish I had the answers.'

'She used to be so happy-go-lucky, Lex.'

There it was again, the way she said his name. It was the way it came out on a whisper that set his pulses racing!

* * *

By the time they reached the stream their conversation had died again.

For some reason Lex had lapsed into a moody silence that Susie didn't know how to break. The brief discussion regarding his family was certainly stilted. Although it might be considered small talk Susie wondered if small talk was enough. Was this new friendship doomed from the moment she'd set eyes on him on Wednesday? Her stomach did a little somersault as she recalled exactly what she saw.

Gloria! In spite of saying he should have mentioned Gloria sooner, Lex actually said nothing about her. Another question that remained unanswered was what his parents said about him going into their shop and seeing her and Mum. Moreover Patsy's conduct was mystifying! Why did she make such an effort with Gloria while being so at odds with Susie and her family?

Lex paused at the same place as yesterday.

'I should have brought a blanket.' He stooped down to put the basket on the bank.

'There's the small one in the bottom of this basket, remember,' Susie said.

As he stood up again, she noticed his cheeks were flushed and she had the distinct feeling he was embarrassed about something.

'No — I mean yes, I do remember.'

By the time the basket was unpacked

and they were sitting on the blanket, a definite silence had settled over them. Concentrating on opening the bag of sandwiches, Susie wondered how to start up a conversation again — anything was better than this awkward silence.

'Oh Susie, cheese and pickle — my favourite!'

'I remembered.' The words tumbled out before she could stop them!

Lex's colour deepened. 'The blanket . . . I admit I'd forgotten. Only it's been such a long time and Gloria always expected — ' He cleared his throat. 'Always expects me to do what she calls 'the manly things' and provide a blanket on picnics.' His breath shuddered. 'She has strong views regarding men's versus women's roles, despite being a career girl.'

Susie's stomach roiled. She shouldn't have agreed to come — he had a girlfriend! She steadied herself — she was overreacting. They were only friends, and tenuous friends at that.

Despite her still somersaulting stomach, she schooled her tone into one of interested curiosity.

'Gloria is a career girl then?'

Taking a sandwich from the bag she proffered, Lex nodded. 'So she says.' He looked at the sandwich. 'It looks delicious. I didn't realise I was so hungry.' He bit into the soft bread.

Annoyance edged through Susie. Was Lex being dismissive of women who wanted careers?

'A career girl?' she snapped. 'What does that mean anyway? Some could say my nan was a career girl. Look at how she started the shop and how my mum's always worked there — and me too.' Susie's annoyance gathered momentum. 'If I continue the tradition, will I be a career girl? Lots of women, married or otherwise, go out to work by necessity — does that make them career girls? What's wrong with a woman wanting a career?'

Swallowing his mouthful of sandwich, Lex stared at her. Why was she getting so worked up over something he assumed would be of little consequence to her? Trying not to appear confused by her outburst he shrugged.

'I think in Gloria's case, she intends to have a career instead of getting married and having a family,' he said.

Susie didn't seem to be able to control herself. 'So a married woman with children who works too isn't considered a career girl?'

Still confused, but not wanting to show it, Lex nodded. 'I believe so.'

Presuming the topic was at an end he took another bite of the sandwich. 'You always made wonderful food. This is delicious!'

Whatever was within Susie that caused her to snap wasn't about to go away and she totally ignored his thanks.

'So a husband and family should be the sole aim of women or they're considered 'career girls' only, not worth a man's serious consideration?'

Lex gulped. 'Surely that's what most

women want, isn't it? A husband and children?'

'Is that all men want?' Susie demanded. 'A good little wife who does as she's told!'

It was as if the food in his mouth turned to ashes as something inside him stretched taut like overextended elastic.

He'd wanted Susie more than she would ever know, and he'd thought the feeling was mutual. Yet after pouring out his deepest feelings in that letter, he never heard from her again! In it he'd told her he wanted to be with her for the rest of his life and would she do him the honour of becoming his wife. She would never know how he'd been on tenterhooks waiting and longing for her return letter.

A letter that never came.

Although his heart seemed to thrash against his ribcage at the painful recollection he kept his voice steady.

'Most men want to take care of the

woman they love so that she doesn't need to go out to work if she doesn't want to. But like your dad and grandad I think it's up to the woman to decide whether to go out to work or not.'

Susie knew she was behaving like a dog with a bone but she couldn't seem to stop. 'So in your opinion, a career woman is someone who doesn't want to rely on a man for support, and is therefore unfit to be married?'

Still puzzled by her hostile attitude, Lex shook his head. 'No, that's not what I'm saying at all.'

He didn't want to quarrel with her but he couldn't understand why she was so het up about the difference between women who chose a career and women who wanted a husband, children and a home.

He knew lots of women who made a career in the RAF, many of whom had little choice after the injury or death of their husbands during the war, except to work. His own mother worked and although they weren't well off, he never felt his mother chose work over them.

All Susie could see in her mind's eye, though, was the exquisitely attractive Gloria done up to the nines in the latest fashion to lure men — her man! Her heart jolted with dismay. Oh no! It couldn't be — she couldn't possibly be jealous of the glorious Gloria, could she?

Then it hit her, and all became crystal clear. She was a fool above all fools. Lex had ditched her for Gloria! Her throat tightened and as she stared at the sandwich in her hand, she knew if she tried eating it, it would stick in her throat like barbed wire. He'd jilted her for another — and a single-minded career woman at that! How could she have been such an idiot not to have realised?

Time seemed to stand still, yet the moment whizzed by too because the next thing she was aware of was him handing her an opened bottle of ginger beer. Dumbly nodding her thanks Susie hoped that taking a sip would ease the tight feeling in her throat.

'It's very fizzy,' Lex warned.

Putting the bottle to her lips, Susie took a tiny sip and immediately started coughing.

'Wrong way,' she wheezed. A second later Lex was patting her on the back. 'Thank you,' she croaked as her throat cleared and she was able to breathe again.

'I told you it was fizzy.'

They ate in companionable silence until they'd finished all the sandwiches.

'Time for cake,' Lex smiled.

It was that smile that made her heart turn over and her spine tingle with those tiny shimmying diamond-clad ballerinas. Ruthlessly quelling all the somersaulting in her stomach, she forcibly reminded herself that he was taken. Career girl Gloria was his intended now!

Nan always said things can change for good or bad in an instant, and that taking the rough with the smooth was part of life.

Fixing a smile she took the bag of cakes from the basket. 'What cakes did you choose?'

'Open the bag and see.'

That heart-stopping smile again! Her spine threatened to start tingling again but an inner voice screamed *Stop!*

'Apple turnovers with fresh cream!'

'I remembered you liked them. I also remember that you love fresh cream meringues but your mum doesn't make those. There's a new coffee shop in Newynn that sells them, though. We'll have to go there sometime and have some.'

Susie thought her heart would flip right over! Had he just asked her to go out with him again? What about Gloria? No — she wouldn't think of his girlfriend because she didn't need to; it wasn't as if it was a date. They weren't a couple any more.

'Sounds great,' she said brightly, 'I'm looking forward to it already.'

His impish grin washed over her. 'Me too.'

They finished off the rest of their picnic with inconsequential chat that Susie deliberately initiated and doggedly kept going so neither of them could mention the past. Although Susie had lots of questions popping into her head, she quashed them. She and Lex were getting on, so they could wait.

'That was wonderful, Susie,' Lex sighed, popping his nectarine stone into an empty paper bag and putting it into the basket. 'We'll have to do this again — soon.' He narrowed his gaze and looked directly into her face.

Susie only managed to resist the urge to ask if that would be before or after their visit to the meringue shop in Newynn by clamping her lips tightly together.

Lex frowned. 'I'll take that pursed-mouth silence as a no then, should I?'

Lex thought his heart would jump through his ribcage, it thumped so hard with disappointment. He'd thought

119

they were making progress but how wrong he was — she looked as if she had a mouth full of lemons!

Holding his hands up before she had time to deliver a scathing retort, he drew a quick breath.

His whole being ached with longing for things to be as they were two years ago when they were in love, a longing that had eaten away at him without him even being aware of it. He'd thought he was over her. Oh, how he had tried to get over her, banish her from his mind and his heart — until Wednesday night when he saw her on the bus.

He was dating Gloria, but he shouldn't date one girl while still in love with another. His heartbeat subsided as he recalled meeting Gloria. It was she who instigated their first date, asked him to take her for a drink during a 'ladies excuse me' at an RAF dance. He could hardly refuse, could he? Besides, it had been months after Patsy told him about Susie and Prand, so he'd agreed.

He was flattered that all the guys

thought the blonde-bombshell with the stunning figure and fluttering eyelashes was the most attractive female in the room. But if he'd still been with Susie, he would have told them all in no uncertain terms that his Susie outshone even the exquisite Gloria.

That first date with Gloria led to others until he found himself going steady with the girl all the other guys wanted. What man could not like the beautiful, clever Gloria? But as he later came to recognise, she was dispassionate rather than serene — no, in fact she was positively icy at times. In company she was sweet and charming, and called him darling, but she was often bossy and critical when they were alone.

Although when they'd first met she'd been adamant about not wanting a husband and children, recently she'd hinted she wanted to marry and have a family. Moreover he had the disconcerting feeling that she expected him to do the honours in proposing. Her very recent interest in engagement rings was most alarming.

Why was he even still with her? Even if Susie wasn't interested in him — and his spirits sank at the thought — he didn't want Gloria. He had to tell her how he felt.

His stomach knotted. Not now, though — not until she finished her exams.

7

Now he'd asked Susie out again and her compressed mouth said it all! He took a consoling breath. 'It doesn't matter, Susie, I get the message.'

He looked genuinely crestfallen and Susie asked in astonishment, 'What message?'

'The message that you're not interested on coming on another picnic with me.'

'What gave you that idea?'

'The way you pressed your lips together and remained silent when I suggested it.'

She didn't want to tell him she'd wondered whether the picnic would be before the tea-shop in Newynn or after. Even if she mentioned it lightly she might sound over-eager — and insensitive, considering he had a girlfriend. Now, though, she had to tell him. She was embarrassed, but was being thrilled that he'd asked her on another picnic reason to feel embarrassed? Why shouldn't friends picnic together?

'I, em . . . ' She cleared her throat. 'I was wondering which would come first — the picnic or the meringues.'

Lex's heart leapt — she wanted to go out with him after all! In spite of his skyward hurtling spirits, he rapidly gathered his senses and reminded himself that as much as he wanted it, they weren't a couple.

'Which would you like to do first?' He wanted his tone to be upbeat and jokey but all he managed was a croaky rasp.

His rich husky tone made Susie's insides feel aerated and frothy and as his blue eyes roved her face, the froth turned to a dizzying fizz! She must not feel like this! He was in love with Gloria — the girl he threw her over for.

'Tea-shop or picnic? Susie?'

Remembering Gloria brought Susie

back to her senses. She glanced upwards.

'I suppose it depends on the weather.' She leaned forward, picked up his empty ginger beer bottle, dropped it into the basket beside hers and stood up. 'I ought to be getting back to the shop.'

Rising, he bent down, scooped up the blanket, gave it a couple of shakes, folded it and put it into the basket which he then picked up. Swinging the basket slightly, he gave a sideways grin that made Susie's insides go all fluttery, and without even thinking what she was doing she linked her arm through his free one. He reacted by squeezing his arm into himself so that her arm was trapped securely by his side.

'Nice,' he murmured, 'just like old times.'

Realising what she'd done, Susie whipped her arm away. Why had she tucked her arm through his in that familiar way?

'I'm sorry.' It came out as a mumble but he heard it all the same.

Coming to a standstill, Lex wheeled round to face her. 'What are you sorry about?'

Having stopped walking, Susie saw from Lex's wounded expression that he was hurt. What was she sorry for, exactly?

'I wasn't thinking.'

He raised a brow. 'You're sorry for not thinking? What were you not thinking that made you sorry?'

It sounded funny, but determined not to be diverted into irrelevant chit-chat, she stood firm and rolled her eyes up at him.

'You know what I mean, Lex.'

An amused smile crossed his lips. 'Do I?' He gave a soft laugh. 'Oh Susie, I do love it when you come over all stern!'

Her heart jumped as a myriad of memories tumbled through her brain. It had always been like this when they were in love. Her heart lurched . . .

when they were in love!

His expression softened. 'Are you sorry for putting your arm through mine? Or sorry that I squeezed it closer to me?'

Not even knowing the answer to that, Susie shrugged and started walking.

★   ★   ★

'You're very preoccupied this afternoon, love.'

Forcing a smile, Susie looked up from the shop display she was arranging. 'Am I?'

'Yes. You've been quiet with customers too.'

'I'm sorry. I hope I haven't offended anyone.'

'I think it's just me that noticed, love,' Gwen said gently. 'Are you all right?'

'Yes, why wouldn't I be?'

'If seeing Lex is upsetting you — '

'It isn't!'

Susie gathered her thoughts. Why

would going on a picnic with Lex upset her? Her stomach fluttered as an intense misery heaved through her. Mum was right, she was upset — and she was in love with a man who had dumped her for the stunning Gloria!

Gwen smiled ruefully. 'Why don't you go and make a pot of tea for Mr and Mrs Rowe? A natter with them will be a nice break, and I can close up on my own.'

A faint smile crossed Susie's lips. Mum believed that doing even the most seemingly trivial good turn for others lifted the spirits. Mrs Rowe would be pleased, and despite preparing to move, she would love talking about old times. Susie knew she, too, would relish a good natter.

★   ★   ★

Coming down the stairs and going through the kitchen door, Susie realised her time spent reminiscing with Mr and Mrs Rowe was time well spent. They were happy and looking forward to their move.

'This place is going to seem so empty when we go, isn't it?' Mrs Rowe mused.

Susie nodded.

'Maybe you could find a use for it,' Mrs Rowe ventured. 'I ran my little dressmaking business from here, remember? I did quite well, even after Smites department store opened.' She looked around. 'I think you'd do very well too.'

Susie swallowed — that's just what Lex had suggested. Having her own business was something she only thought of, but never really believed could ever happen.

'Apart from running the shop I wouldn't know what to do,' she sighed. 'The shop does all right because everyone knows us, but what business could I run? I wouldn't want to be in competition with Mum, and she isn't ready to retire.'

'You'll find something,' Mrs Rowe said.

Suddenly Susie jumped at the sound of her dad's voice in the kitchen. She was so preoccupied she forgot he was home early on Fridays. She hurried downstairs in answer to his call.

'I took some tea up to Mr and Mrs Rowe.'

Dad took the teapot from her. 'I expect they're looking forward to their move.'

Susie watched her dad empty the cold tea from the pot, rinse it and put in a fresh lot.

'That reminds me, somebody's asked if they can rent the flat.' He said it so nonchalantly that Susie wondered if she'd imagined it. He glanced up. 'What do you think?'

Too stunned to reply immediately, Susie stared at him, then gathering her scattered senses she puffed out an indignant breath. 'Would whoever it is jump into their grave as quick?'

'Susie!' Dad blinked. 'What a thing to say!'

They were standing by the wooden

draining board next to the cooker as the kettle began to whistle. Snatching it up, Susie yanked off the lid and sloshed the water into the teapot.

'That'll be boiling,' her dad reminded her.

Susie knew that! Resisting the urge to tell him she wasn't a child, she thrust the kettle back onto the cooker.

'Tom Prand,' Bernie continued in the same nonchalant tone he used before mentioning the water. 'The letter I received this morning about renting the flat is from him.'

It was lucky she wasn't still holding the kettle because the juddering shiver Susie gave would have caused hot water to slosh all over her!

Bernie frowned. 'Goodness, you're jumpy! First it was my voice, now it's the idea that someone wants to rent the flat.' He lowered his chin. 'Is everything all right?'

'No, everything is not all right!' Just mentioning his name aloud made her blood curdle! 'Tom has a home and a family. Nan let the flat to Mr and Mrs Rowe because they were in dire straits! The least we can is honour Nan's memory by waiting until someone less fortunate comes along! *And*,' the words kept tumbling out, 'although Mr and Mrs Rowe kept it in pristine condition, it still needs some updating.'

'Updating?' Bernie chuckled. 'Like on one of those American shows that have latest gadgets, the most modern furniture, and a shower over the bath?' Bernie became serious. 'I can't deny it, love, a tenant would make the place feel more like home, but who wants a little place like that these days?' He answered his own question with, 'Only someone in need.'

'Well it would have to be someone in real need.' Remembering what Mrs Rowe and Lex had suggested, Susie added, 'It has business potential, too.'

Bernie's eyes widened. 'Business potential?'

There was a protracted silence between them before Bernie spoke again with a thoughtful tone.

'How do we know Tom isn't in need? Mum tells me you're dead set against him. Is there a reason for that? Something I should know?'

Susie's insides knotted as an inexplicable thick frosty darkness slid through her, but she shook her head. 'No.'

'Then why are you so tense whenever he's even mentioned?'

The thick frosty blackness obscured her reasoning and blanked her brain.

'I don't know, Dad. It's just that he's . . . ' Not knowing how to explain that he gave her the heebie-jeebies, she paused. 'He's . . . too forward.'

'Too forward? How?'

'Well, he comes here on Wednesday nights and asks about me.'

'But you aren't here on Wednesdays, so how is that forward of him? Surely asking after you is only polite?'

Wanting to finish the subject of Tom Prand without making an issue of it, Susie looked at the teapot. 'I think the tea's ready.'

The front door opened and closed. 'Just in time,' Bernie winked as Gwen came through. 'The tea is brewed, even though you're early.'

Relief from the subject of Tom Prand!

'I had help from Roy Sawson, the young man who came yesterday,' Gwen explained.

Sorry he hadn't found work, but pleased he'd come again, Susie smiled. 'Did you load him up with goodies before he left?'

'Yes, and I found out that he *is* the boy we talked about yesterday, the one banned from several Oldwynn shops.'

Susie's spirits fell, yet there was something else disturbing her too. Was he one of the gang Patsy hung around with? She hoped not!

'Do you think he targeted us?'

'I don't know, but I'm sad for him now that I've met him. It's so sad that his dad wouldn't let him go into the RAF for his National Service. He's so eager to help.' She nodded to Bernie.

'And he helped me make up the grocery orders.'

Bernie looked at Susie. 'That's our cue to get going, love.'

* * *

Later on, enjoying a Friday supper of fish and chips after finishing the grocery rounds was one of the highlights of the week. This Friday was no exception, but as they ate, something entered Susie's mind. 'I remember Nan always loved Friday night fish and chips,' she said.

Gwen shot Bernie a curious look. 'Do you? You've never mentioned it before. You've never mentioned Nan or Grandad since they died. It was as if you buried all your memories of them.'

Bernie shot Gwen a warning look.

'Well, it's true, Bernie.' She turned to Susie. 'We tried to understand because we've known since you were little that you lock unpleasant things away and never mention them. Remember the dog from next door but one?'

'Gwen, don't . . . ' Bernie warned.

Something broke open in Susie's mind.

'Yes, he was the fluffy golden retriever with a feathery tail that never stopped wagging. He was called Dems and got run over by a lorry on the main road.'

She took a breath and wondered why it still hurt after so long — especially as she hadn't consciously thought of him from that dreadful day.

'He had to be put down as there was nothing anyone could do, but you never mentioned him again. Not even to ask where he'd gone.'

'I didn't need to ask, I knew.' Susie toyed with a chip. 'I knew where Nan and Grandad had gone too. I occasionally dream about them.'

Bernie frowned. 'You've never said.'

Susie was confused. What was all this about? Why had mentioning Nan liking Friday night fish and chips become a big deal all of a sudden?

'And Dems, sometimes.' *And Lex,* she nearly added, but suddenly she felt peculiar and cross inside. 'Not mentioning things doesn't mean I've completely forgotten them.'

'We know that, love.' Bernie was gentle.

'Am I supposed to talk about things that upset me all the time?'

'No, darling.' It was an endearment her dad used in times of greater concern. 'It's just that we worry that you lock difficult issues away.'

'The doctor assured us it was normal and that maybe you would talk about difficult issues later without feeling traumatised,' Gwen added.

Susie glared at them both. 'How can I be traumatised by things I hardly remember?'

Her parents looked at each other.

It was a silly conversation and Susie couldn't think why never talking about traumatic events was a problem.

'What sort of things are in your dreams?'

Susie pulled a face. 'I don't know, Dad.' She felt irritated. This was a fuss over nothing! 'Nothing of importance. I remember dreaming about them, that's all.'

A mischievous smile crossed her dad's face.

'Mum kicks me in her dreams!'

Gwen gave a hearty chuckle. 'I do not, Bernie Cotting, you terrible man!'

Looking from one to the other, Susie smiled, partly because it was funny and partly because her dad always knew how defuse a tricky situation either by changing the subject or saying something funny — and he'd just done both.

'I was only pulling your leg.'

'First you say I use my leg to kick you in bed, and now you're pulling it,' Gwen riposted. 'It's a good job I'm a dutiful wife and remembered to bring in the ice cream in from the shop freezer.'

Grinning with appreciation, Bernie nodded. The subject of Tom wanting the flat was dropped, Susie's dreams about Nan forgotten, and even the subject of her going on another picnic with Lex wasn't brought up.

★ ★ ★

Later that evening Bernie entered the back living-room with a tea tray.

'Did you bring in the custard tarts?' Dad grimaced and Susie stood up. 'I'll get them.'

As she came back into the room Gwen beamed.

'Oh lovely, custard tarts. Tom left them for us.'

Bernie shot her a warning look.

Forcibly banishing an icy chill, Susie carefully put the cakes on the coffee table, and attempting to not over-react levelled her eyes at her mum.

'When did he bring them?'

'He came to inquire about the flat while you and I delivered the groceries, love,' Bernie said.

'I don't know why you are so against him,' Gwen countered. 'He's polite, and seems keen to branch out on his own. The flat would be ideal for someone like him.'

Bernie held up a quelling hand. 'Gwen love, it hasn't been discussed properly.' He turned to his daughter. 'Anyway, Susie has plans for it.'

'What plans?' Gwen quizzed. 'I don't know what's wrong with having Tom — or anyone else for that matter — living above the shop.'

It wasn't the 'anyone else' Susie minded. It was the thought of Tom being so close by that gave her the creepy-crawlies!

'Lex wondered if I might turn it into a dressmaker's,' she blurted out. Then huffing in a breath, she added with more self-possession than she felt, 'I've had a few business ideas actually.'

Gwen pulled a face. 'What sort of business ideas? Not floristry, I hope? You know pollen gives me the sneezes! If you turned the place into a florist shop I'd be out of business within a week.'

Bernie groaned. 'Ladies, please. Susie has no intention of becoming a florist, and Susie, the matter of letting the flat has barely been discussed, let alone decided, and your idea of using it for business premises only came up today.'

This was getting too out of hand and she was making it worse by over-reacting! At the same time however, she wanted to scream and yell and throw a wild tantrum just so they'd realise how strongly she felt!

She did neither. All she said was, 'I don't want a custard tart, thanks.'

* * *

The comedy on the television made her parents laugh, but all Susie thought about throughout the evening was Lex. The thing was, no matter how much she tried, her inner psyche dragged her mind back to him and her time with Lex hurtled back.

When Dad chuckled at the TV, it reminded her of the way Lex chuckled.

When Mum sighed over the shows, that too reminded her of how Lex sighed. Her mind kept going over and over their conversations to such an extent that she could recite every word, envisage every nuance, and see every gesture.

What would it be like to be with him all time? What would it be like to kiss him again?

At this point her heart skipped a beat as her treacherous brain reminded her that right now he was with Gloria!

8

It was Susie who got up to make their night time drink. Her dad followed him into the kitchen. 'You all right, love?'

Susie put the milk in the pan while he got out cups. Not wanting him to see any sadness or longing in her face, Susie's eyes roved everywhere in the kitchen except at him.

Noticing, Bernie sighed.

'Yes, it definitely needs updating, doesn't it? I realised when we talked earlier that it's about time we had a re-fit in here. Those modern appliances will make life easier.' He indicated the work top next to the sink. 'One of those up-to-the-minute all-singing, all-dancing washing machines.' He looked over to the far corner. 'I've seen adverts for those domestic fridges with a large compartment for freezing food in.' He smiled. 'I like the idea of that.'

It was inconsequential chat and Susie suspected he was staying clear of the subject of the upstairs flat. A thought crossed her mind however — was he also hinting that if the flat was rented out, they could afford a new kitchen for themselves with all the latest gadgets?

Although the thought niggled and part of her felt guilty, she forced a smile. Was she being selfish not wanting the flat to be let out? After all, Mum worked hard in the shop then came home and did most of the chores too, so Dad had a point. Even so, the idea of letting the flat out to pay for a kitchen that looked like a magazine page still made her feel miserable.

'Mum's happy with this kitchen,' she said.

'Yes, but I suspect there's a part of her that longs for something modern and less time consuming.' He turned to glance at the clock. 'Like that old thing for instance. It never keeps proper time. We need a new cheery red one.'

Susie wanted to chivvy him away

from the subject. 'How do you know this new stuff is red?'

'There's a trade magazine at work that advertises all kinds of things.'

'Why now, all of a sudden?'

Bernie smiled self-consciously. 'A friend at work is buying a brand new house in Newynn that he's raving about. His wife is over the moon about the showhouse kitchen. She's insisting on the full works — a new electric cooker with a double oven, one of those big fridges, and a washing machine that does everything in one go that's plumbed into the water system. Imagine that!' He chortled. 'He says their house will look like a television stage set!'

Susie took in their tiny kitchen in one glance.

'It must be a huge kitchen to be full of that lot.'

Dad nodded. 'Probably, but with a few tweaks, we could fit in a washing machine and a fridge.'

Happy at the thought of her mum

having an easier life, Susie threw her arms round her dad. 'You're a wonderful dad to me and a wonderful husband to Mum. Have you mentioned it to her?'

His eyes twinkled. 'Yes, and what's more I'm taking her out to see *Gigi* to celebrate.'

Susie let him go. 'That's great! When?'

He became serious. 'That depends, love. If you think you'll be fine on your own in the shop tomorrow afternoon, I'll take her to the early showing, then onto somewhere for supper. If not, it'll be tomorrow evening.'

Despite the tiniest apprehensive jolt Susie grinned at him. 'Of course I can manage alone.'

Bernie frowned, 'You don't mind spending an evening on your own, either?'

'I'm not a child any more.' Susie smiled. 'I'll buy a couple of magazines and curl up on the sofa or watch television.'

'It's hardly the way for a youngster to spend Saturday evening.'

Relieved he didn't mention that Lex might take her out, but miserable that Lex hadn't asked her, she drew a controlling breath. 'I insist, Dad.'

★   ★   ★

Gwen was humming and flicking a duster across the shelves as Susie entered the shop the following morning.

'I can tell you're looking forward to your date with Dad,' Susie said.

'A date?' Gwen laughed. 'I think your dad and I are too old to be dating, don't you? The very expression 'dating' is far too modern to be applied to us.' She gave the shelves a final flourish before glancing at Susie. 'When are you seeing Lex again?'

'Mum!'

Shocked at her mother's train of thoughts, Susie couldn't control her feelings, especially after the vile and frightening nightmares she'd been having!

'Mum, Lex and I aren't dating!' All the same, just the mention of his name in the context of dating made her spine dance with those shimmying ballerinas again. 'Besides, you know he has a girlfriend, Mum, because I told you that only yesterday!'

Looking abashed, Gwen visibly swallowed.

'I'm sorry, love I didn't mean it like that. I didn't mean to imply . . . well, you know . . . '

Feeling guilty at her outburst and her mum's resultant discomfiture, Susie softened her tone. 'Well, I suppose arranging an outing in advance can be seen as making a date, but it's not actually dating . . . '

'The same but different,' Gwen laughed.

That made Susie laugh, and her mum's faux pas and her own horrible night were forgotten.

'I think Roy will be round this morning.'

Susie pulled a face. 'You do? Why?'

'I asked him to come and help.'

'Mum! I can manage on my own.'

Gwen shook her head. 'I didn't mean because I won't be here. I asked him yesterday, before I knew about going to the cinema.' She drew a breath. 'When I mentioned money though, he said a few groceries would be enough.'

Trying not to dwell on her mum implying that she and Lex were dating, Susie concentrated on the list of customer orders being collected before the shop closed.

Last night, before going to sleep she had found herself wondering and imagining what it would be like living in a brand new house with all the most modern labour-saving gadgets with a TV advert red and cream kitchen. She had even imagined it — and her heart skipped a beat again at the thought — with Lex as her husband!

Yet even those pleasant musings hadn't prevented the hideous dreams from plaguing her. They seemed to be getting worse and she didn't know why. There were more threats, more whispered insinuations, and more raucous laughter. But they weren't real.

She dragged her mind back to her task.

An hour later, Susie was back to her cheerful self as young Roy shyly entered the shop and took off his battered cap.

'Mrs Cotting told me she needed help this morning, miss.'

'Yes.' Susie beamed at him. 'She's just popped up to make the Rowes some tea, but she said the windows and ledges could do with a clean inside and out — if you'd like to do that?' She watched a shy smile cross his face. 'Then lunch and bringing the vegetables in when the shop closes at three.'

Her heart went out to Roy! He was so willing that he didn't even want money for his work; groceries were enough. What a coincidence that he happened to walk past at the exact time she was taking the vegetables in that day!

⋆   ⋆   ⋆

'That's a great improvement,' Bernie called out after parking his van round the back.

The dishevelled Roy looked up from cleaning the front window and grinned. 'It wasn't that bad to begin with, really.'

'It's still a big improvement.'

'Thanks,' Roy said and continued cleaning.

Bernie whistled in time with the tinkling doorbell. 'That's that done for another week.'

Gwen was busy with Mrs Shottle and didn't look up.

Susie was wrapping up bread and grinned at her customer. 'Dad loves doing the rounds.'

The customer smiled. 'It's that young man out there we're interested in. We were only saying yesterday that we need a good window cleaner round here. Just

151

look at him polishing!'

Mrs Shottle put her cherry Bakewell in her bag.

'I think he'd be perfect for the job.'

Not wanting to reveal what she'd heard about Roy, Susie nodded. Maybe he could get regular window cleaning work? It might not be what he'd had in mind, but work was work.

Bernie beamed at them. 'That's an excellent idea! I think something can be arranged. I'll ask him about it when he's finished.'

'We can put an ad in the window,' Susie said.

'I think a notice is a good idea,' Mrs Shottle agreed. 'But once word gets around I doubt it'll be needed.' She turned back to Bernie. 'In the meantime we'll put the word out.'

A thread of excitement whipped through Susie at the thought of poor Roy being able to earn a decent living at last.

'I think that's a lovely idea,' Gwen said after putting money in the till. 'I think we can all recommend him and put a notice in our window.'

As the two women left, Susie heard Mrs Shottle whisper rather too loudly, 'What a difference seeing that Lex Maceul again has made on Susie.' Susie's stomach knotted. Goodness, that woman didn't miss a trick, did she?

'Are you staying for some lunch, Roy?' Bernie asked as the last of the vegetable crates were brought in. 'It's just a snack of soup, sandwiches and a slice of cake today.' He grinned at Gwen. 'Because my sweetheart and I are having a slap up dinner later on.'

'Thank you, Mr Cotting.' Roy seemed glad to be invited and Susie was pleased her dad asked him. The poor lad looked as if he was half starved.

'Dad's home-made soup is wonderful,' she told him, smiling. 'And it'll be ham sandwiches and Mum's golden crunch cake to follow.'

Her mind instantly whipped to Lex. Mum's golden crunch cake was his

153

favourite! *Stop!* an inner voice screamed. *He has a girlfriend!*

'And as much tea as you can drink,' Gwen added happily.

'Sounds like a feast.' Roy grinned.

Pushing her thoughts of Lex aside, Susie found herself wondering why he used that word.

'Well, it's hardly a feast, Roy.'

'It is to me,' he replied as they made their way to the house.

★ ★ ★

Saturday afternoons were usually quiet, as many of the women went into town to either browse or to buy.

'The corner shop won't last long,' Bernie often sighed. 'Those bigger shops will soon be selling everything under the sun.'

'We'll be retired by then,' Gwen always countered amiably. 'So it won't matter to us.'

'It'll matter to folk who can't get out and about,' Bernie usually replied.

It was true, things were changing. After years of shortages, Wynnton and the new shops in Newynn were bulging with goods. More to the point, people had more money to spend on them. In spite of what Lex said about career women, more and more women were going out to work.

Mrs Shottle regularly announced that one of her daughters had started demonstrating the latest electrical appliances in a store near her, and not only loved it, but made good money too. Another was selling kitchenware by going into people's homes. It sounded just like the sales method Lex mentioned. Susie secretly wondered if Mrs Shottle would be quite so approving if it wasn't her own daughters.

Susie sighed. Two years ago, all she wanted was to be with Lex. Nothing else mattered, but now, as the prospect of the unlived in flat loomed, the idea of turning it into a business venture was becoming more appealing, although she was worried her skills would not be up to scratch. Something else, perhaps? What about having a showroom kitchen put in and demonstrating how everything worked? She sighed. She would need a supplier and money for that.

She watched Roy as he finished the last of the inside windows. He could soon be doing this on a regular basis. Yet if a woman wanted to clean windows she would be frowned on — but why? Why were there such rules regarding the roles of men and women?

She remembered what Lex said about Gloria and that she expected him to provide a picnic blanket because it was a 'man's job'. Ignoring the anguished jab of her insides at the thought of Lex and Gloria on a picnic together, Susie wondered why tasks were set like that — did it really matter who did what?

'You've done a great job, Roy,' Bernie said as he discussed the prospect of a window-cleaning round during lunch. Although Roy had previously thought about labouring, he seemed keen to follow the window cleaning idea.

'Once the word spreads, I think you'll do very well,' Susie assured him. 'And we have some ladders you can use.'

'I'm grateful to be given a chance, Miss Cotting,' he replied.

Susie chuckled. 'Please call me Susie.'

Roy blushed and went outside to start his task of bringing the vegetable display boxes inside.

Susie then put a large empty box on the counter, and began placing a few groceries in it.

As Roy came in with the last crate, she grinned.

'I believe you and my mum agreed on a few groceries,' she said to him. 'So you'll have to tell me what you want.'

'What I want?'

'Yes,' Susie paused. 'Or would you rather just have the money?'

Roy looked aghast.

'Oh no, just the leftovers — if that's all right?'

'Roy, you've worked all day and Mum said you were to have what you want. I'm filling up this box with groceries, so you can either choose or I'll have to guess what your mum might need.'

Just then the door-bell tinkled and as Lex suddenly bounded into the shop Susie's heart skittered with joy at the sight of him!

'Hello, Susie.' Then he saw Roy. 'Oh — it's Roy Sawson, isn't it?'

'He's been doing some work for us.'

'I see,' Lex grinned.

'He's worked really hard so Mum says he's to choose some groceries.' She turned back to Roy. 'How about I suggest things and if you and your family like them, they can go in the box?'

Roy nodded and Susie began filling up the box for him to take home.

Lex vaulted the counter and began taking tins from the shelves and placing them in the box. 'Let me help.'

Susie eyed the glass counter, then

looked sternly at Lex.

'Sorry,' he grinned. 'I'll go round it next time.'

Roy shook his head as Susie and Lex put groceries into the box. 'That's too much,' he protested.

Lex chuckled. 'I can assure you Susie will know when to stop.'

Eventually the shop door tinkled again as Lex held the door open for Roy. 'Mind how you go, and make sure you hold the box from underneath.'

Susie watched Roy as he loped off with the box while Lex turned the sign to *Closed* and slipped the latch on.

Lex couldn't let Susie see how affected he was by her and her parents' generosity to Roy which brought the memory of that amazing Christmas flooding back again! But what had he and his family done to make Susie and her family turn against them the way they had?

As far as he could see, nothing had changed. All he knew was that Susie had stopped writing to him then Patsy told him Susie was going out with Prand. Just thinking of the man made him fume!

As he turned to face her, the words tumbled from his mouth before he had time to think.

'Do you ever see Prand these days?'

Susie's jaw dropped and for a moment she couldn't think, let alone speak. All she could remember was that once Tom asked her to be 'his girl' and she refused. She had a vague sense of a vitriolic and threatening tirade of vile abuse from him, but her mind had shut it away even before she walked off.

'I avoid him if I can.'

'Avoid him, why?'

Susie's stomach churned. 'When Patsy started hanging out with his gang I used to go because . . . ' She paused and swallowed back the memories. 'Well, because Patsy wanted me to, but I didn't like being around them so I stopped.'

'Does he ever come in to the shop?'

'Yes.' Why was he asking all these questions?

'So you can't avoid him then.'

'No, but I don't chat to him either.' Susie purposely turned her attention to a leftover cake. 'This won't last so I'll take it to the stream for the ducks. Do you fancy a walk down to the stream?' She could have bitten her tongue! Why had she invited him to go with her?

Lex raised an eyebrow. 'I'd love to but I wondered if you'd like to go to that tea-shop I mentioned, the place in Newynn with the meringues?'

She flushed and his heart fluttered to see it.

Susie knew she was blushing, yet there was an old warmth and familiarity between them that felt so right.

'Yes!' Why had she been so eager? 'I mean . . . that would be lovely,' she amended in a calmer, more modified tone.

Lex looked at his watch. 'The next bus is in fifteen minutes. Think we can make it?'

'I'll hurry,' she grinned. 'Come on round, and I'll be ready in ten.'

Susie had already planned to wear her turquoise and cream polka-dot dress for their tea-shop outing. It was the very latest fashion and she'd made it herself for Easter. Mum always said Susie had a good eye for fashion, and Mrs Rowe often praised her creative flair.

Fifteen minutes later they arrived panting and laughing at the bus stop just seconds before the bus arrived. Lex was in a daze of happiness. It was such a joy just to be hand in hand with her like old times. How could it be like this? How could his memories race back and fill him with exhilaration one second, and then pour cold desolation and bleak despair over him in the next?

9

They got on the bus laughing, but Susie's heart had thumped the moment she noticed the appreciative longing in his eyes when he saw her after she'd got changed and ready! Every nerve in her body shimmied and danced with the thrill of seeing him standing in the stippled light of their back sitting-room, his skin glossy with desire.

She knew if he moved towards her, took her in his arms with soft murmurs of tenderness and need, she would not refuse him. She would have given everything there and then for his love. She wouldn't have given Gloria another thought. She wouldn't care that they weren't even engaged and that no promises were made. She loved him!

He didn't, though. Instead, his expression changed, he imperceptibly relaxed and the pulsating, electrifying atmosphere changed.

'It's been a long time since we ran for a Saturday afternoon bus,' he panted.

Susie, with a swirl of her dress, made straight for the top. Her heart fluttered and her spine quivered and danced as Lex's steadying hand touched her waist. Ignoring the delicious inner dancing, Susie scoured the top deck, saw two spaces together and — just like old times — made straight for them. Lex followed.

As they sat down, the person in front looked round. Susie's stomach knotted and Lex tensed.

Tom Prand!

'Where are you two off to?' Tom smirked.

Lex and Susie spoke at once. 'Newynn.'

Lex was more forthcoming. 'For tea and cakes at that new place.'

'Really?' Tom blinked in mock surprise. 'I was just on my way there myself. He hesitated. 'I'm thinking of taking my mum there for her birthday.'

Susie thought he was clearly fibbing when he added, 'I want to find out if it's any good first.' He smirked directly at Susie, 'What a happy coincidence, I'll tag along if you don't mind?'

Susie did mind! What could she say to deter him without sounding impolite?

'We might be a long time.' She hoped she didn't sound bad-mannered. She would hate Lex to think badly of her.

'We can take as long as you like,' Tom breezed. 'I have all afternoon.'

Susie could feel how taut Lex was.

'I find it difficult to believe you're going to Newynn late on a Saturday afternoon just to go to a tea shop,' Lex declared in rigid tones.

Tom laughed mirthlessly. 'Do you? I find it hard to believe that you're taking a girl other than your fiancée out to a tea shop.'

Engaged? Lex never mentioned that! Susie's breath hooked into her throat like jagged barbed wire. It constricted and narrowed her airway causing her voice to sound metallic and sharp rather than mildly surprised.

'You didn't tell me you were engaged.'

'Susie Cotting, whose family own an old-fashioned corner shop and know all the gossip for miles around, didn't know that Lex Maceul was engaged to the glorious Gloria Somebody-or-other?' Tom sneered, 'How amusing!'

Although inwardly reeling, Susie noticed the stormy blue of Lex's eyes.

'I am not engaged to Gloria,' he said in sibilant but vehement tones.

It was obvious from his smug expression that Tom was enjoying this. 'That's not what I heard.'

Lex surged forward. 'And just what are you implying, Prand?'

Knowing Lex was upset, Tom immediately turned away from them.

Susie's brain rallied and she put her hand gently over Lex's. 'Leave it.'

Lex looked down at Susie's distraught expression. Fighting for his pride wasn't worth it if it hurt the girl he loved. A rush of emotion raced through him. Oh, how he still loved Susie!

'I'm not engaged to Gloria,' he repeated.

'Lex,' she managed softly despite her pounding heart and barbed-wired throat. 'It's alright. I know we're just friends and that's all. Whether you're engaged to Gloria or not, there's no harm in us being friends.'

They heard Tom give a scoffing laugh, but he kept his back to them and didn't speak again for the rest of the journey.

However, he followed them to the tea-shop and plonked himself down at the table nearest to theirs, so their conversation was stilted.

Susie and Lex stayed in the tea-shop as long as they could and after ordering their second pot of tea Tom had clearly had enough. He paid his bill and left.

'That's a relief,' Susie whispered.

Lex scoured her face. 'How did it end?'

'How did what end?'

Lex held her with his gaze. 'You and Prand, how did it finish?'

'Me and Tom?' The hairs on the back of her neck rose and chilled. 'Why on earth would you ever think I could go out with him?'

As bafflement slackened her features Lex began to wonder if Patsy had got it really wrong.

Then Susie shuddered. 'I have never been out with him, but apparently he's interested in me.'

'How do you know he's interested in you?'

'Mum says so.'

As Lex studied Susie's face, he realised the colour had seeped from her cheeks.

'Are you all right, Susie?'

Without warning Susie jumped from her chair and raced from the tea-shop.

'Wait!' was all he managed before realising the waitress needed to be paid.

By the time Lex caught up with Susie she was at standing at their bus stop.

'Susie, what's wrong?'

Lex now knew that implying she and Prand were ever a couple created an adverse reaction in her. Anger engulfed him and his fists balled, but as her gaze glided over his face and he saw it was steeped in pain, he forced himself to relax. If Prand had hurt her he would deal with that later, but right now, he had to listen to whatever it was she had to say.

Without thinking he reached out and gently stroked her cheek. His whole being heaved with the longing to draw her towards him her hold her close and never let her go.

Susie felt embarrassed. Why did she run off like that? Why did she keep making an issue of Prand? Her stomach knotted, and despite all intentions to the contrary, her voice was sharp.

'Why do you keep mentioning Tom Prand with the insinuation I went out with him? He even wants to rent our flat — and it's your fault!'

'My fault?'

Aware of others waiting for the bus, Susie tempered her tone. 'If you hadn't mentioned letting out the flat, Tom wouldn't have applied.'

As his concern washed over her, her exasperation and anxiety drained away and was replaced by a glowing affection.

She had to be strong!

Noticing the softening of her expression, Lex took her hands in his, drew then up to his mouth and gently brushed his lips across them.

'I don't think I mentioned it to anyone.' He paused. 'Maybe to my folks, but that's all.'

His folks! The family who hated hers? What gave him that right? Snatching her hands from his, she glared at him. 'Well, it seems your folks must have spread it around!'

Lex blinked at her in surprise. 'I may have mentioned it in passing. It certainly wasn't a discussion, though.'

Susie knew she was being unreasonable and in spite of her feelings regarding Tom, Lex didn't deserve a scolding. Her anger subsided.

'I'm sorry, Lex.' She swallowed before continuing softly, 'I don't know why you think I ever went out with Tom, but I can assure you that I haven't — and never will.'

Glancing up, Lex took her hand as their bus juddered to a halt at the bus stop.

'I get that loud and clear now . . . though why Patsy thought you were is beyond me.'

Susie jolted in sudden shock.

'Patsy said I was seeing him?'

'Yes, after I sent you that letter.' Lex took a deep breath as they boarded the bus. He paused, took another breath and cleared his throat. 'Patsy wrote telling me not to bother contacting you again as you were seeing Prand. Naturally I wrote to you asking if that was true — and then twice more after that — but I never got a reply. What was I to think?' His heart heaved at that dreadful memory

171

of seeing her and Prand together.

Susie's heart pounded as they made their way up to the top deck then to the front seat.

'Why would Patsy do that?' It was only when Lex's eyes narrowed that she realised she'd thought aloud. 'She told me I was a troublemaker and that you and your family never wanted to speak to us, and that we weren't to contact you ever again.'

Lex stared at her. 'She told us *your* family never wanted to see or speak to us again. We asked her why, but she said she didn't know. Mum wrote to your parents to ask what it was about but got no reply.'

Susie's throat tightened so her voice was sharper than she intended it to be.

'My parents got a letter from your mum saying we were a disgrace and she never wanted to have anything to do with us again! Mum sent a letter back, but she got no reply from *your* mum.'

Shocked, Lex stared at her. Something in her bewildered expression, the set of her jaw, the tiny crease between her eyes told him that she was telling the truth.

Susie tried to understand what had happened between their families. What made Patsy turn against them? Why did Beattie Maceul send Mum that letter, then deny getting one back? Why did Patsy lie to Lex?

Something Lex had said caught up with her.

'You said 'that letter' . . . What letter?'

Lex was too deep in thought too hear her. Then he suddenly leaned over and kissed her.

Her stomach whirled, her limbs felt weightless, her brain was frothy, yet her eyelids were deliciously heavy! This was meant to be! As he pulled softly away, a vague chill blew over her.

His eyes, deep and dark like mystifying lagoons roved her face.

'Sorry, what did you say?'

'The letter you sent to me?'

His eyelids dipped and rose as

though drenched in liquid silk, but her question brought him back to the present.

'It was the letter I sent asking you to marry me.' The memory of that time rampaged painfully through him and he raked a hand roughly through his hair. 'I know that writing to you wasn't as romantic as asking you, but I was about to be posted and knew I wouldn't see you at Easter as we'd planned.' The words throbbed through him. 'I needed to know if you truly felt the same way as I did before I asked Bernie . . . ' His voice faded to a whisper. 'I never heard from you again . . . '

Susie's stomach turned double-somersaults. 'Oh, Lex — ' She swallowed to fight back the emotion threatening to overwhelm her. Lex had proposed! For a split second her spirits danced with dizzying joy. Just as rapidly however, her soul sank with hollow disappointment. 'I never got that letter. After falling-out with Patsy I never heard from you again. I wrote to you, but you never replied. I never saw you again until I saw you at the bus stop with . . . ' Susie gulped. 'With Gloria.'

Lex saw and felt her anguish.

'Susie darling, I don't know what to say but I have a horrible feeling Patsy could be to blame for all of this. I know she's been weird for a while, but I had no idea it was this bad.'

Silence lingered between them, a contemplative quietness allowing each to ponder their thoughts and recent discoveries.

'I wonder if Patsy was jealous?' Lex eventually ventured, more to himself than to her. Then he looked at Susie. 'Of us and our future?'

Susie mulled it over for a moment.

'I never thought of her as a jealous person. She was always so happy-go-lucky and looked on the bright side of everything . . . but maybe she was secretly jealous of what you and I had and I didn't know.'

Poor Patsy! What kind of a friend was

she that she didn't know of Patsy's distress?

'I'm sorry to have to say this about her, but she did some terrible things, Susie. This could mean that she . . . ' He shuddered. 'No, she wouldn't. Would she?'

His desolate manner made Susie want to hug him tight and her mind momentarily blanked. 'Wouldn't what?' Susie's stomach knotted as she got his meaning. 'You think she wrote the letters to our parents?'

'Oh, yes, that too, but I was thinking of the letters we sent that neither of us received.'

An appalling thought slammed into her. 'You think she intercepted our letters, got rid of them?'

Lex closed his eyes as his breath came out in shudders. 'I sincerely hope not.'

He looked so wretched that Susie reached out to him. Taking both his hands in hers she felt the same fizzing sensation she felt when their fingers touched when they'd both swished them in the stream. Her spine danced with tiny shimmying ballerinas that made her nerve endings tingle and her heart pound — but this wasn't the time!

Managing to curb her exhilaration, she shook her head trying to concentrate on the serious matter in hand. Oh, how she loved him!

'Darling, don't think too badly of her. If she was jealous, maybe we can include her more?'

Lex's heart raced. Did Susie know what she'd just implied — and also that she'd called him darling? He came to his senses with a shattering crash. Gently clasping her hands, he frowned.

'It's a criminal offence, Susie. Interfering with post means she'll be prosecuted.'

All the euphoria abruptly ceased as Susie's stomach coiled into tiny, tight springs.

'No, we can't let that happen to her, Lex.'

His face clouded. 'It won't be up to us.'

'Can you speak to her about it? Tell her you know and see what she says?'

'You mean in the hope that our correspondence was the only one she interfered with?'

'Well, yes — because if they were, nobody needs to be any the wiser, do they?'

His eyes roved her face and Susie felt every part of her melting under that lingering gaze. She mustn't read anything into those searching looks he gave her. She mustn't let him see that her feelings were any more than that of friendship.

Yet two years ago he'd wanted to marry her! Oh joy! But then her happiness plummeted . . . he was with Gloria.

⋆　⋆　⋆

As the bus neared Willbob Street Lex smiled. 'There's new a burger bar in

Wynnton.' Despite needing to get to the bottom of the Patsy problem, the truth was that he couldn't bear to let her go so soon. 'It's got a juke box with all the latest songs . . . do you fancy going?'

In spite of the tea and cakes, and in spite of her turbulence regarding Gloria and Patsy, Susie's heart fluttered. 'I'd love to.' She tried hard not to appear too keen, yet felt so happy being with him.

Once off the bus, Lex took her hand as if their break-up had never happened. All thoughts of Gloria and Patsy subsided.

As they strolled hand in hand into the burger bar, a group of girls sitting round a table stopped chatting and turned to look at them. Trying not to feel annoyed, because after all Lex was the best-looking guy in the place, Susie went and sat at the only empty table while he ordered burgers then put some money into the juke box.

After he slid into the seat beside her,

Susie heard the girls having a whispered discussion . . .

'I can't do that.'

'Yes you can.'

Trying to ignore them, Susie turned to Lex.

'It's busy in here.' But before he had time to reply, there was a voice behind her.

'Excuse me.' One of the girls, looking slightly abashed, smiled. 'We love your dress!'

So it was her dress and not Lex they were fascinated by? 'Em . . . thank you.'

The girl blushed. 'I know this sounds a bit cheeky, but where did you get it?'

'I made it.'

'She made it!' The girl called back to her friends. All the girls swivelled towards her.

'We're third year design-school students. Where did you get the idea?'

Mildly embarrassed, Susie shrugged.

'I don't know. I make most of my own clothes.'

'You could make a fortune. Everyone's looking for designs like this.' She pointed to the girls. 'We designed a student collection fashion show. The audience loved it and we got one or two orders. At the insistence of our tutor, we took the collection to Smites and asked if we could showcase them there, but they turned us down.'

Susie was sympathetic. 'That's a shame. They'd probably do well in their private fashion shows, especially in the evening when they supply refreshments. But maybe their range caters for women who like traditional clothes.'

The girl raided her eyes. 'Traditional? Old-fashioned, more like! Lots of our friends love our work but they can't buy them in the High Street. We thought about opening a shop, but it's so expensive in Wynnton, and Newynn isn't practical. It isn't expensive to put on a show in design school, but we only get a limited number of people who come. We thought about hiring a hall, but really we need a less formal venue.'

Lex cleared his throat. 'Smites probably got their sales-party ideas from America. The women their invite their friends into their home where a sales person demonstrates the products. When the invited women place orders, the demonstrator gets a commission, and the hostess gets free products based on the sales amount. A hostess will often sign up to be a demonstrator and so it goes on. It's supposed to be a terrific way of building a business.'

While delighted that Lex was interested, Susie thought that mentioning American 'party-sales' wasn't helping — besides, according to Mrs Shottle it was tableware and cosmetics at those party plans.

'I've heard about those,' the girl sighed. 'But I'm not sure anything like that would work for us. We'd need a decent place to store our collection, then we'd have to convince our friends to have parties, then they would have to convince their friends to have parties . . . '

'So all you need is a place to store and show the collection?' Susie's mind was buzzing . . .

10

Susie uncurled her legs and, brushing her thoughts aside, glanced up from the magazine she'd been trying to read for the last half-hour. All she could think of was being with Lex and then the conversation with the students.

'Did you enjoy the film?' she asked her parents as they entered the room.

Bernie smiled. 'Yes indeed.'

'Then we had a lovely supper in The Crown afterwards,' Gwen added.

Susie stretched her legs and put the magazine down beside her.

'You look as if you had a comfortable evening.' Bernie gave a rueful smile. 'Did you know there's a new burger bar in town with a juke box?'

Susie's stomach skittered with pleasure. Her spirits wheeled and soared, not just because of spending the afternoon with Lex, but also the ideas she had about the fashion design students she'd spoken to.

After Sally the student in the burger bar handed her a piece of paper with her telephone number, Susie's ideas had steadily grown. Was there a way to help them — and her — by starting up a business, but what would it take to do so — and would her parents agree?

Her mum's voice brought her back to the present. 'We were just saying that maybe you and Lex should go next week?'

Bernie shot her look. 'I never mentioned Lex.'

Suddenly Susie was trying to curb the excited thumps behind her ribs. She mustn't give anything away by grinning too much. Yet some of the words of Paul Anka's new song *You Are My Destiny* that Lex had played over and over on the jukebox reverberated through her head once more.

Lex had seen her to her front door and she wasn't sure if she was pleased or disappointed that he'd respected her and her parents too much to spend any time alone in the house with her and hadn't attempted to kiss her again. However, part of her was proud of him for being the gentleman he was.

Gentleman or not, her insides still fizzed with excitement and her spine still shimmied with diamond-spangled dancers as she silently relived her afternoon.

Pushing aside her exhilarated thoughts, Susie managed to school her face and her voice into composure. She would tell her parents about her afternoon with Lex and their date for the following Saturday another time.

For now she wanted to bask in her happiness without her parents misconstruing the situation.

'I'm glad you had a lovely evening,' she said.

'Yes, it was wonderful,' Gwen sighed happily.

'Perfect,' Bernie added.

'You should arrange a special date

night on a regular basis,' Susie suggested.

Her parents laughed.

★ ★ ★

'You all right, love?' Bernie acknowledged Susie with his usual morning greeting.

Her nod was as casual as she could make it.

'You look a bit pale.'

'I have a slight headache, that's all.'

He turned back to the bacon he had sizzling under the grill.

Susie never wanted to worry him by mentioning her nightmares. Besides, she wasn't sure if she could remember everything. Sometimes she slept all night without dreaming, but for the last few nights her dreams gave her cause for concern. Were her parents right — did she lock traumatic events away?

'When are you going to put a security light up by the back gate?' she asked.

Bernie swung round.

'Is something worrying you, love?'

'Why?'

'Asking me about the security light was a bit random, that's all.'

Susie didn't know why she was even thinking about the security light. 'Yes, I suppose it was.'

★ ★ ★

The rest of the day was spent helping the Rowes pack the last of their belongings. Thankfully the constant reminiscing kept Susie's mind off her upsetting dreams, but it didn't prevent her from pondering the Gloria and Patsy situations that suddenly took precedence over the events of the previous afternoon.

Yesterday, being with Lex was all she could think of, but now, troubling thoughts centring around Patsy and Gloria were on her mind so much that she nearly blurted it out several times, only just managing to stop herself by focusing on the packing.

Later on though, once all was finished and she and her parents were in their back sitting room again, Susie's mind returned to the situation.

A soft silence had threaded through them as her dad was reading his paper. Her mum, absorbed in her knitting with the pattern on her knee, kept sighing.

At last she spoke. 'I'll miss them.'

Bernie looked up. 'I know, but it's for the best.'

Grateful the silence had broken, Susie perked up. 'There are lots of lovely new shops in Newynn now, so they'll be able to do more for themselves.'

Gwen and Bernie frowned in unison. 'When did you go into Newynn?' Gwen asked.

The thoughts of what Patsy may have done and what she'd spent all day trying to quash hurtled back. Taking a deep calming breath, she smiled.

'I went yesterday with Lex.'

Gwen stopped knitting. 'You went into Newynn with Lex yesterday and didn't mention it to us? Is it a secret?'

'I didn't mean not to mention it, Mum. I just didn't get around to it, that's all. It's not a secret.'

Part of Susie felt guilty at not saying anything, but the suggestion that it was a secret was annoying. She was just about to say that she wasn't a secretive type of person when she remembered her Wednesday evening class.

'I was going to tell you sometime.' That was true. 'If we hadn't been busy upstairs, I would have told you today. It's no big deal. We're just friends, after all.'

Well, if that was true, why was her heart pounding, and why did she seem weighed down and yet light and frothy at the same time? What was happening to her?

'I didn't tell you last night because I was interested in your evening.'

'Susie, do you think . . . ' Bernie looked at Gwen as if he needed help but she stayed silent. 'Well, what I'm trying to say is that when things ended badly between you and Lex, you were devastated. I don't want you to go through that again. I want you to be happy, love.'

Susie looked at him with dismay. 'Do you disapprove of Lex?'

'No, of course not,' Bernie sighed, 'I just don't want you to get hurt all over again.'

'You said again as if it's happened several times over.'

'Bernie, we were all hurt,' Gwen said quietly. 'That business with the Maceuls had a shattering effect on us all.' She shook her head. 'I still wonder what we did to upset them.'

Susie inhaled a deep sigh as silently as possible. She wanted to explain why it happened, yet for Patsy's sake she dared not.

Then there was also Gloria. Her heart skittered as she remembered that she and Lex had kissed and what it felt like to be close to him again. She wanted to tell them the way his eyes pooled to dark blue lagoons and the gentleness of his touch. All she said was, 'He has a girlfriend, remember?'

'Yes I saw them together at the bus stop on Wednesday,' Bernie responded dryly.

'You never said,' Susie responded.

Gwen whipped her face to Bernie and shook her head sharply in silent warning. Taking the cue, Bernie went back to his paper.

*   *   *

Susie couldn't settle. She wished her dad had told her about seeing Lex and Gloria together earlier; his telling her now made it more real somehow. Moreover, the situation regarding Patsy writhed within her.

When her mum mentioned the Maceuls she should have told them everything immediately. Knowing the fall-out was down to Patsy rather than anything the family had done made a lot of difference. Perhaps it would help them if they knew Beattie and Len were just as confused about the situation as they had been?

At the same time however, telling her parents might mean having to mention the letters Patsy may have taken, which might mean formal investigations.

Susie's throat felt dry and rough as she pondered it all yet again. Notwithstanding all that had passed between them, she couldn't bear the thought of Patsy getting into trouble, so she had to be sure of Patsy's involvement before flinging accusations around. It was all such a mess!

'You know you can tell me anything, don't you, love?'

Susie's mum didn't miss a trick.

Looking into her mum's face Susie drew a breath. 'Of course I know I can tell you both anything, but sometimes — ' she tried not to sound upset ' — I have to work things out on my own.'

She took a deep steadying breath, then leaned over and placed a gentle hand on her mum's arm.

'It's not just about Lex, Mum, and it's something I can't discuss with anyone yet.'

'Have you got big problems on your mind?'

'No, not really,' she reassured. 'I just need to sort some things out on my own and once I have . . . ' Then what? 'Once I've sorted it all out in my own head, then you'll know all about it.' Pleased with her reply she smiled. 'Don't look so concerned — I'm all right, I promise.'

Gwen nodded. 'I can't help worrying, love, but I know you have to make your own decisions.'

Susie suppressed her roiling emotions, pressed her lips together, and wished it was time to turn the television on.

★ ★ ★

Lex was about to go upstairs when Patsy, throwing a cardigan round her shoulders, came clattering down.

'Going somewhere?' he asked sharply.

'I may be,' Patsy retorted in a tone that implied Lex was intruding. 'What's it to do with you?'

Ignoring her hostility and knowing how touchy Patsy was, Lex refused to be ruffled by her belligerence. He needed to talk to her calmly so the last thing he wanted was to antagonise her further.

'Mind if I tag along?'

She reached the bottom stair.

'Yes, I do, as it happens.' She barged past.

'Got a hot date?'

Patsy's dark hair bounced as she swung round to glare at him. 'No.'

'So there's nothing to stop me accompanying you, is there?'

'I don't want company — that's reason enough.'

Lex saw she was rattled but he really needed to talk to her and as this was the first and possibly only opportunity, it had to be now.

'Can't a brother and sister be friends?' Lex persisted.

'Why be friends all of a sudden?'

Lex took a step back. 'We used to be friends once, why can't we be again?'

A look of anguish crossed her face so briefly, Lex wondered if he imagined it.

'That was a lifetime ago.'

'I really need to talk to you.'

Patsy swallowed, 'I can't right now.' She shrugged. 'Later, perhaps.'

Lex was determined. 'I'm coming with you.'

'You are not!'

Throwing open the door, Patsy raced into the street. Lex dashed after her. She was being silly. She knew she couldn't outrun him, so why attempt it? He caught up with her and managed to catch hold of her arm and bring her to a halt.

The impact of being brought to a sudden standstill sent an envelope slithering from under her arm onto the pavement and before she had time to do anything, Lex swooped down and whisked it up.

'That's mine!' Patsy tried to snatch it from him. 'Give it to me!'

Lex held it out of her reach so Patsy lunged at him. She might have knocked him to the ground if he wasn't agile enough to dodge backwards. Darting back gave him a chance to glance at the name and address on the letter.

'Gloria?' He held the letter too firmly in his hand for her to get it. 'Why all the cloak and dagger stuff?'

'There's no cloak and dagger stuff as you so dramatically put it. Hand it over!'

Lex almost gave in. After all, he knew Patsy and Gloria corresponded, so why all the fuss? Yet something niggled at him.

'Why didn't you just say you were going to post a letter to Gloria?'

'Because it has nothing to do with you!'

'I'm not saying it has, but you could

have told me anyway. You're behaving as if it's a secret.'

He paused to look at the envelope then narrowed his eyes.

'You do know that Gloria's on a course and she won't be at this address for six weeks?'

A look of dismay crossed her face. 'Oh.'

Pushing aside his curiosity at her reaction, Lex shrugged. 'If you'd asked I could have told you before you wasted money on a stamp.'

Patsy gave an indifferent flutter of one hand. 'One measly stamp doesn't matter.'

Her rapid change from agitation to nonchalance didn't fool Lex. He knew she was still on edge but he really had to talk to her.

'If you still want to post Gloria's letter, I'll walk to the letter-box with you. As I said I need to talk to you.'

Before she had time to respond Patsy glanced up and as Lex followed her gaze he saw someone ambling towards them from the direction of the post box.

Lex spoke without thinking.

'Where'd he suddenly spring from?'

Patsy glared at Lex. 'What do you mean? Why did he have to have sprung from anywhere? Why can't he be taking a Sunday afternoon stroll?'

Given her behaviour of late, the hostility of Patsy's tone shouldn't have shocked Lex, but it did nevertheless. Was his dislike of Prand so evident that she felt it necessary to defend him with such ferocity?

Not wanting to make it obvious that Patsy was in a mood, Lex pushed the envelope into his pocket. He remained amiably silent as Prand sauntered up to them.

'Hello you two.' Prand merely glanced at Lex before settling his gaze directly at Patsy. 'Fancy seeing you here.'

Patsy addressed Prand directly. 'I was just going to post a letter to . . . ' She threw Lex an odd look. 'To Gloria,

Lex's intended. However Lex insisted on escorting me to the post box.' She looked at Lex. 'Didn't you, big brother?'

'Goodness me,' Prand grinned at Lex. 'Twice in twenty-four hours. Makes one wonder if the Fates have a hand in things.'

'Yes, and that's twice I've seen you without your gang in tow.'

Prand flinched slightly. 'My gang, as you call them, aren't glued together.' There was an infinitesimal pause. 'We have completely separate lives and what they get up to in their own time has nothing to do with me.'

Ignoring Prand's adamant tone and Patsy's faint whoosh of breath, Lex aimed for conciliation rather than provocation.

'It's a good job I did catch Patsy before she posted her letter to Gloria.' He threw Patsy a withering look. 'Since Gloria — who is not my intended, by the way — isn't currently at the address on the letter and won't be back there for six weeks.'

'She's on a course,' Patsy added.

Was that relief in her voice? Lex studied her for a second but her expression was bland. How was she able to manage such rapid changes of attitude and facial expression within seconds? One moment she appeared to be full of animosity, then nonchalance, then relief, then nonchalance again!

Prand snickered. 'How lucky for you Patsy. Your dear brother can tell you her present address so you can rewrite the envelope.'

Patsy stared at Prand for a moment. 'That will make a mess of the envelope!'

Her rapid change surprised Lex yet again.

Prand chortled and held out his hand. 'Just give the thing to me and I'll do it then!' With his other hand, he reached into his trouser pocket and produced a ballpoint pen.

Lex felt Patsy stiffen, yet her tone was firm.

'I'll take it home, put it in another envelope and send it tomorrow morning.'

'Just give it to me, Patsy!'

'Lex has it.'

Prand glowered at Lex. 'Hand it over, Maceul.'

The air prickled with tension as Lex looked from Prand to Patsy.

'I think Patsy's idea is better. Besides I don't know her address offhand. I'll have to look it up.'

From the look on Prand's face Lex thought there might be a tussle for the letter, although he couldn't for the life of him see why Prand would take it upon himself to intervene in this way.

'As you wish,' Prand finally shrugged, putting the pen away and glowering at Patsy. 'Don't say I didn't try, Patsy.' With that he swept past them and stomped off.

Baffled, Lex stared at Patsy.

'What was all that about?'

A brief expression of indignation crossed her face, then was gone.

'I don't know why you think anything is wrong. I'm going home.'

'Why don't we go for a walk?'

'No, I need to rewrite the envelope ready for posting tomorrow.'

'I'm sure it'll get forwarded if you send it as it is. It'll just take a bit longer, that's — '

'No!' Patsy didn't give him time to finish. 'I need to get it to her as soon as possible.'

Since leaving the house Lex, too, had gone through several emotions. Now he felt a mix of curiosity and concern.

He knew he could outrun Patsy and be back at the house before her then go into his bedroom, lock his door and open the letter. That really wouldn't be a kind thing to do, though, would it?

Her current calm, though, was having more of a troubling impact on him than all her tantrums put together.

'Patsy?' He gently touched her arm but she instantly snatched it away from him. 'Patsy, if there's anything wrong, anything worrying you . . . ?'

'Why does everyone seem to think there's anything wrong? Why does everyone make such a big fuss about me wanting a little privacy?'

That did it! Something in Lex twanged and without another thought he was off, racing away from his sister as fast as he could.

It was only as he reached Susie's front door that Lex realised where he was going. Glancing briefly back to see if Patsy had followed him, he knocked loudly.

It was Bernie who answered.

'Mr Cotting,' Lex panted, 'I need to see Susie.'

★   ★   ★

Shocked, Susie stared up at Lex.

'We can't, it wouldn't be right,' she said.

They were alone in the front sitting-room so there was nothing to stop them, but Susie still felt uncomfortable about what he had suggested.

'I know, but her behaviour was so bizarre I don't know what else to do.' He shuddered. 'Then there's your suspicion about her intercepting our letters — and maybe even sending letters to both our parents. You have to admit that it makes this look suspicious as well.'

'But two wrongs don't make a right, Lex.'

A bleak expression crossed his face.

'I know, darling, but perhaps we need to intervene this time — if only for her own good.'

Susie's spine was suddenly shimmying with euphoric delight as the spangled dancers twirled through every nerve of her body — he had called her darling!

No — this wasn't the time! She drew herself back to the letter, wondering if Lex was right.

Lex inhaled deeply.

'I'll open it. It isn't just curiosity, I'm concerned too. So much so, that I wouldn't be surprised if Patsy guesses

I'm here and turns up demanding to be let in.'

Susie doubted that Patsy would. After all she hadn't been near the place since their row.

'Surely the letter is too insignificant for that?'

'That's just it though, Susie — the way she was behaving makes me wonder if this letter is more important than we could ever imagine.'

Worried about doing the wrong thing, yet knowing Lex had a point, Susie reluctantly agreed.

They both sat on the sofa and nervously looked at the letter . . .

11

Susie stared unseeingly down at her hands. 'Why?' she whispered more to herself than to Lex. 'Why would Patsy write that?' She couldn't look at him because there were too many unanswered questions racing like agitated moths through her mind.

Why was Patsy so against the Cotting family. Why had Patsy written such a letter to Gloria? She thought of his kiss on the bus yesterday and wondered again — what was Gloria to Lex?

Lex put an arm round her and drew her to him.

'I have no idea, darling.' His shudder went through her. 'I only know that I never stopped loving you.'

Susie's stomach fluttered as she looked up into his face. 'You didn't? You really didn't?'

His eyelashes looked as if they'd been

dipped in liquid silk. 'No, I didn't.'

Only then did the worrying question slip out.

'What about Gloria?'

Lex frowned and rubbed his forehead. 'Now I realise I was never in love with Gloria.' He stopped rubbing to look directly into her face. 'I know I sound like a complete rogue, Susie, and I'm not proud of myself for my behaviour but I suppose I was flattered by her attention. I know that's no excuse but she seemed to like me and . . . and, well, you didn't.' He looked away from her. 'I know that's no defence.'

Susie's stomach rolled from fluttery and tingly to tight and coiled.

'Did you . . . did you tell her you loved her?'

Lex turned to her again with a grave expression. 'There was a time when I believed I could grow to love her.' He closed his eyes for a moment before murmuring, 'But I knew deep down that it would never happen.'

Susie's stomach coiled like tiny springs that wound together and formed knots in her stomach. She didn't want to know the details, she didn't want to hear about Lex and Gloria together . . . yet her mouth opened and the question rushed out.

'When did you know for sure that you didn't love her?'

Lex had a bleak look and swept his hand over his face, swallowing hard.

'I knew the second I saw you on the bus on Wednesday that it wasn't going to work between Gloria and me. But I knew way before that too, because after a while the things I initially liked, admired and respected about her became the very things I didn't, and never would, find attractive.'

'Such as?' Again Susie's mouth opened before she had time to think.

His eyes scoured her face. 'Susie . . .' His voice dropped to a troubled whisper. 'I'm sure you don't really want me to run her down and talk ill of her, do you? Can't I just say that once I discovered we wanted different things, I knew it wasn't going to work? There were times when — and I'm ashamed to admit this — when her attitude irritated me.'

Susie couldn't control the need to know. Was it Gloria wanting a career that irritated him?

'Irritated you in what way?' she persisted.

He sighed. 'I can't tell you that, Susie, we both know it wouldn't be fair. Though, I suppose irritated is too strong a word to use. I guess I was puzzled by her manner rather than irritated. For instance she was dead set against me meeting her folks, and I only ever met one of her friends.'

'Maybe she was ashamed of her parents?'

'She said very little about them. Maybe she was ashamed of me?'

Susie bristled. 'Ashamed of you? How could any girl be ashamed of you? You're the kindest most wonderful man a girl could ever meet. You're loyal, dependable, hard-working . . . ' She felt herself blush but went on nevertheless. 'And you're the best looking man on the planet — and what's more, I love you!'

'Oh, Susie!'

He gently cupped her chin and tilted her face up to look at him before he bent closer to her and gently grazed her mouth with his.

As his lips brushed hers her whole body seemed to slide into a silky, soft eiderdown. Her spine went all shivery — thank goodness she was sitting down because she knew if she was standing she might have collapsed due to her knees feeling all weak!

Suddenly it was over as Lex rapidly drew back.

'Susie,' he rasped. 'I'm so sorry.'

Still in a tingling daze all Susie did was look at him. Why was he sorry?

He moved as if he was about to stand up but she caught his hand. 'Please don't be sorry.'

Lex briefly rubbed his free hand over

his face before looking at her again.

'I wanted to speak to Gloria before any of this. Since yesterday though, especially after discovering that it might be Patsy's doing, I haven't stopped thinking about us and the possibility of our future together.'

He took her hands in his. 'And thinking about our kiss . . . ' His eyelids fluttered with a delicious silky languor. 'And how I feel when I'm with you . . . '

He gave her a brief despairing look. 'Susie, I'm hoping there's a chance we can start over . . . please tell me there's a chance we can put the last two years behind us and start afresh?'

Susie tried to ignore the effect his nearness was having on her but failed. She felt shaky and fragile. However, at the same time she felt strong and powerful. But lurking in the background was pain . . . what about Gloria?

'I would like that more than you could ever know,' she said softly.

'Oh, my darling Susie!'

He leaned toward her, and this time his lips didn't just graze hers, he kissed her — gently at first, then as she responded, his kiss intensified and all the shimmying fluttering spangled diamond-clad dancers twirled and pirouetted through every part of her body!

When he drew away, the midnight velvet of his irises slowly receded and returned to a sumptuous cobalt blue.

Then the muscles in his cheeks contracted as he shook his head slightly and groaned.

'I don't know why Patsy is doing all this.' He picked Patsy's letter to Gloria up from beside him. 'This is a lie beyond belief.'

'It's obvious Patsy wants Gloria to come hurrying back.'

'Yes.' Lex glanced briefly at the letter before tossing it back beside him again. 'What is difficult to understand though, is why.'

Susie's heart thumped with misery.

'She doesn't want us to be together, Lex.'

'But to lie like that? To write to Gloria saying I've been knocked down by a car and am seriously injured and lying in hospital begging to see her?' He shook his head. 'What if Gloria had dropped everything and suddenly turned up?'

'You said she isn't at her usual address.'

'No, but I'm sure the letter would reach her eventually — and right in the middle of her course, too.' He paused. 'I have to admit though that her being away for six weeks gave me a strange sense of relief.'

He squeezed her hands. 'And before you ask — yes, that was before I saw you on the bus. I don't want her hurt any more than necessary, though. You do understand that, don't you, Susie?'

Susie did understand, but what she didn't want to think about was how long it was going to take.

'I suppose you'll have to tell her face to face.'

Lex nodded. 'Yes, I will.'

'Is it possible for you to go and see her before you go to North Coates?'

Lex let go of her hands and stood up.

'I'll have to, Susie. I love you and I don't want us to be a secret.'

Susie's heart surged with love for him.

'I love you too, Lex.'

Suddenly in one smooth rapid movement, he was kneeling in front of her.

'Susie.' As he took her hands in his, Susie trembled all over. 'Susie, my darling, that's twice you've said that. Is it really possible that you still love me?'

Could he hear how hard her heart was beating? She nodded as her eyes filled with tears and managed to whisper, 'I never stopped loving you.' She gulped back the lump in her throat. 'I thought I had. I tried to stop loving you, tried not to think about you every waking moment but even though I managed to convince my parents I was over you, my heart never let you go.'

Lex swallowed hard. 'I know how I feel, Susie. I know there will never be anyone else for me.'

The breath he drew was deep and reassuring.

'In that last letter, when I asked you to marry me, I knew that writing it wasn't the most romantic way to ask, but I was going away and I wanted you to know how I felt before I left.'

He squeezed her hands slightly then smiled so softly that Susie's heart seemed to turn right over in her chest.

'So, Susan Henrietta Cotting, will you do me the greatest honour in the world by marrying me?'

Susie felt as if she could fly to the moon and back in a trice, she was so ecstatic!

'Yes!' Her voice was hoarse with emotion. 'Oh Lex, yes!'

'Susie . . . ' was all he managed because Susie pulled him towards her and, holding him close, she kissed him with deep intensity. It was a kiss that held all the promise and passion of a lifetime of love to come. Susie couldn't let him go! Not now, not ever! Nothing would ever come between them again!

At last he drew away from her enough to whisper, 'I've dreamed of this moment for so long, my darling, my Susie.'

Dazed and happy and not even wanting to curtail that wonderful shimmying feeling, Susie slid her tongue over her still tingling lips.

'So have I — ' and before she could finish her sentence they were kissing again.

★ ★ ★

After kissing some more and talking some more, Susie and Lex finally emerged from the front room and went into the kitchen where Gwen was filling a teapot.

'Ah — hello, you two. I was just

going to take you in some tea and cake,' she chuckled.

Lex dramatically put his hand to his chest.

'Oh, if only I'd known,' he said with mock disappointment, 'I'd have stayed in there.'

Gwen flushed and laughed.

'Flummery, Lex Maceul, flummery.'

Smiling, Susie glanced up at him. Just seeing Lex in their kitchen bantering with her mum like old times made her heart skitter with joy!

Gwen pursed her lips in wry amusement.

'I see nothing's changed.'

'Actually Mum, something has changed . . . ' Susie looked at up at Lex. The look of pure love she gave him almost made Lex melt — almost.

'I have to do something. Please excuse me.'

A moment later he was gone.

'What was that all about, love?' Gwen asked.

There was a lump in Susie's throat

and her heart was beating so hard it was a wonder her mum couldn't hear it. Lex had planned to wait until things were sorted out but she knew from the look on his face exactly what he was doing right now. She swallowed.

'I think he's gone to ask Dad something.'

Gwen put the teapot with slow deliberation onto a tray. 'Oh, I see . . . '

'Mum, you needn't look so worried. It's all been sorted out.'

Gwen was pensive. 'Susie . . . ' she paused and sighed. 'Don't you think things are moving a little too fast? I don't really think half an hour is enough time to sort out whatever differences you have, do you?'

A niggle of guilt wriggled through Susie. She should mention Patsy's suspected involvement but Lex hadn't spoken to her yet. Surely Patsy deserved a chance to explain before anyone else found out? After all, there might be a simple explanation. Patsy might not have interfered with their letters or written to both sets of parents pretending to be the other. She may not have contributed to anything untoward at all.

There was the letter to Gloria, though, wasn't there? Did that prove beyond all doubt that Patsy was involved in trying to split up Susie and Lex?

'I don't think there were any differences,' she ventured, 'Not really. We think . . . ' she hesitated.

She shouldn't mention Patsy until she admitted it or there was proof and it was being sorted out in a reasonable way.

'We think our letters went astray,' she said at length. 'Lex moved around quite a lot at the time so it's possible that he missed a letter from me, then I missed a letter from him. And perhaps any subsequent letters got lost in the post.'

She knew it didn't sound right, but added, 'These things happen.'

'But if that's the case . . . ' Gwen put four cups onto the tray. 'Why didn't he come and see you when he came home on leave to sort it out?'

Susie's heart bounced. 'He thought I didn't want to see him.'

'So he started going out with . . . ' Her mum's wry expression made Susie's stomach knot slightly. 'With that . . . ' She cleared her throat. 'That girl.'

'Mum, her name is Gloria, and Lex didn't start seeing her until after we stopped writing.'

'After *he* stopped writing, love — and you only have his word for that.'

Why was her mum suddenly against Lex? Susie wanted to vehemently protest against her mum's suspicious attitude and declare in strong confident tones that Lex was wholly innocent, but doing so would only lead into further discussion about why, and how, and so on — until Patsy's name inevitably came up.

'Lex and I have talked it through, Mum.' She purposely kept her tone soft.

'I presume he's packed up with Gloria, then?'

Susie's stomach clenched slightly.

'Not officially, not yet at least,' she admitted, more calmly than she felt.

'So he's two-timing her — and you?'

Susie felt as though she'd been kicked in the stomach by a mule.

'No!' She modified her tone. 'He intends to tell her it's over as soon as possible.'

'How serious was it, exactly?'

Susie shrugged. The truth was that although Lex said he realised he had never really loved Gloria, he hadn't actually said how serious their relationship was.

'Well? Was it serious, Susie?'

The implications of her mum's questions whacked into Susie.

'I believe he was flattered by her attentions,' she faltered. 'And I know there was a point when he thought he could grow to love her but . . . ' Recalling their conversation, she paused before adding, 'He realised early on that they wanted different things.'

'Different things?'

'Well, she's a career girl,' Susie sighed, knowing in her heart that it shouldn't matter — and, more importantly that she was disappointed that it had seemed to matter to Lex.

Gwen was annoyed. 'Are you telling me that Lex doesn't want a career woman for a wife? That he's so locked in the past he wants a woman who's happy to spend the rest of her life cooking and cleaning up after him and his future children?'

She re-arranged the cups on the tray in a way that revealed her indignation.

'There are women out there who spent their war years carving out a career,' she went on angrily. 'And I can assure you, those women were loath to give it up — some didn't! Do you think I would have countenanced your father telling me I couldn't work in Nan's shop? No, I would not!

'Your father's willingness to help out, his willingness to accept that his meals

223

aren't always ready when he comes in — even that he often has to cook for us all — is all proof that he's happy having a wife who runs the corner shop — a wife who is a career woman!'

In her stride now, Gwen would not be stopped.

'Your nan too . . . could she have built up a small business if your grandad had objected to a career woman?' She paused and levelled her gaze at Susie. 'There was a time when you talked about going to train for something, for a career. Admittedly you weren't sure what, but you wanted to all the same.'

Appalled at the way the conversation was going and dismayed at the strength of her mum's feelings, Susie blinked. Yes, after she and Lex finished, she had talked about training for something, but she didn't have a clue what, and didn't even know where to start.

'So Gloria wants to be a career woman.' Gwen plonked a sugar bowl onto the tray. 'So what?'

'Mum that's not what I meant at all.'

Susie stopped talking. After all, hadn't she had the same debate with Lex just a few days ago? And hadn't she too felt het-up and as frustrated as her mum was now? Why wouldn't Lex want his wife to have a career?

'No,' she said in a quieter tone, 'I know what you mean, but I think there was more to it than that, Mum. Besides, while I do think of you as a businesswoman — and I know Dad is proud of you and your work — but you still come home and do most of the chores, don't you?'

Hoping the conversation was at an end, Susie got out the milk jug.

Gwen however was like a dog with a bone now and wouldn't let go. 'More to it? Like what?'

Susie was at a loss.

'Mum, I only know what Lex told me about her being a career woman, and until he said it, I'd never thought about what being a career woman actually means. Besides, I'm not sure I want to know all the details about Gloria.'

Susie's stomach was churning into tight knots. She knew Lex wanted her, and that was the most important thing.

'Of course there's a part of me that wants to know all about her . . . you know, what she was like, and . . . and . . . ' She drew a deep breath.

'No.' She held up her hand as her mum drew a breath to speak. 'Lex always behaved like a perfect gentleman with me. You and Dad knew that and trusted him completely.'

'People change, love.'

A fear that coiled into tight knotted springs gripped Susie's insides, but brushing the feeling aside, she forced herself into composure.

'Mum, I'm the one he loves,' she said, but inside she was in turmoil. *Patsy! Oh Patsy, what have you done?* she cried silently.

Just then Bernie strolled into the kitchen.

'Susie, love.' His tender smile poured over her. 'I need to talk to you.'

Leading her into the front room he closed the door behind them. Although still tenderly concerned he didn't waste any time as he said, 'I'm sure you know what Lex has just asked me.'

Susie nodded.

He took her hands in his. 'What I need to know is how you feel, Susie.'

'I love him, Dad.'

Bernie's gentle gaze poured over her again. 'I understand, love . . . but are you sure? I mean, are you absolutely sure that he and this Gloria are well and truly over?'

Susie tried to ignore the knots in her stomach and the conversation she'd just with her mum.

*   *   *

Gwen had joined Lex in the back sitting-room.

'Congratulations.' Her voice was soft and whispery, and it was as if her conversation with Susie never took place. 'Congratulations to you both,' she said.

Bernie chuckled. 'I think this calls for a small glass of something I keep in the sitting-room cabinet for special occasions.'

'And Sundays,' Gwen laughed.

As Susie and Lex locked hands, Lex bent down and whispered, 'If I'd known where his stash was, I might have toasted your acceptance there and then.'

Giggling, Susie gave him a little nudge.

'Oh lovely,' Gwen said as Bernie came back with a bottle of rosé wine and four glasses.

'I noticed there's a gang out there messing about,' Bernie said as he put everything on the coffee table.

Susie's stomach suddenly turned to ice.

'I heard a noisy kerfuffle outside in the street and caught sight of them jostling around when I got the drinks.' He shrugged. 'I don't suppose it's anything serious.' He poured a little sparkling rosé wine into each glass and handed them round. 'No doubt just kids shoving and pushing and jostling each other along the street.'

Lex shrugged. 'Just a bit of youthful messing about, I expect.'

Susie's stomach was still icy, but she took the glass her dad gave her. 'Thanks,' she smiled.

'I'll go and close the curtains in a moment — what the eye doesn't see, and all that.' Gwen took a tiny sip of her drink, then held up her glass and beamed at Susie and Lex. 'We don't want anything to dampen this happy moment, do we?'

Bernie held up his glass 'I'll drink to that! And to Susie and Lex, of course.'

'To Susie and Lex,' Gwen echoed. 'May they have the same happiness as we have, Bernie!'

'Hear! Hear!' Bernie agreed.

Their celebrations were suddenly interrupted by a loud knocking at the front door. Gwen put her glass down.

Bernie did the same and hurried into the hallway.

Both Lex and Susie placed their glasses of rosé next to Gwen and Bernie's and waited. Within moments Bernie appeared in the room with a police constable.

'Are you Mr Alexander Maceul?' the policeman asked solemnly.

Lex seemed to stand to attention.

'Yes, sir.'

'In that case . . . ' The constable bowed his head a little. 'You had better come with me. There's been . . . ' He cleared his throat. 'There's been an accident.'

12

Susie's heart hammered; an accident that Lex was being summoned to? She was beside him in an instant.

Lex frowned. 'An accident?'

'I'm coming with you,' Susie told him.

'And you are?' the policeman asked.

'His fiancée.'

If it wasn't for the severity of the situation, Susie might have sounded happier but that knotted feeling in her stomach quelled all jubilation.

Had Beattie or Len been taken ill? Oh, dear goodness, had Patsy done something awful?

'Who's involved in the accident?' Susie asked.

The policeman looked at Lex. 'Is this young woman your fiancée, Mr Maceul?'

Gently taking Susie's hand in his,

Lex looked down at her.

'Yes.' He then gestured to Gwen and Bernie. 'And these good folks are my in-laws-to-be.'

The constable shifted his feet awkwardly. 'In that case Mr Maceul come with me for a moment and I'll tell you what it's all about. Then you may use your own discretion as to whether you tell your fiancée and her family.'

Letting go of Susie's hand, Lex followed the constable out into the narrow hallway.

As he disappeared it was as though each one of them stood absolutely still and held their breath to create a collectively orchestrated silence, until Lex finally returned. He stood in the door frame filling the space with his sombre presence.

'It's to do with Patsy. I have to go.'

'I'll come with you, Lex.' Susie was frantic.

His troubled blue eyes roved her face.

'No,' he murmured, 'I have to go alone.'

Susie's stomach knotted into tight lumps as a myriad of terrible and frightening thoughts whizzed around within her.

'Please tell me, Lex — is she hurt? Did she — ?'

Lex held up his hand.

'She's at home. Thank goodness she's safe, but I have to go.' He swallowed so hard that the sound seemed to ricochet round the room as he included them all with one solemn glance. 'If I can get to the phone box I'll call you later, but if I can't I'll come round sometime tomorrow.'

As he hurried away, Susie ran after him.

'Lex!' He turned and she called out, 'Whatever it takes, whatever we can or can't reveal, we have to do what's best for Patsy. Her peace of mind and her safety are more important than anything.'

A moment later he was hugging her

so tightly she gasped.

'Oh, my darling Susie, I love you so much.'

His cheeks were pale when he let her go.

'I may as well tell you that she was found face down in the stream and nobody's sure whether it was an accident or not.'

The policeman just outside the door coughed, and Lex took his leave.

Susie returned to the back room and taking a deep reviving breath, declared more bravely than she felt, 'Mum, Dad, there's something I need to tell you . . .'

★   ★   ★

Much later as they all sat looking at each other, Bernie sighed. 'It doesn't seem right turning on the television after all that, does it?'

'No,' Gwen agreed quietly. 'I couldn't possibly enjoy *Sunday Night at the London Palladium* now.

Enjoying myself in the slightest seems inconsiderate under the circumstances.'

Bernie's shoulders rose and fell. 'I feel the same. I don't feel like laughing, no matter how good laugher is for the soul.'

Susie wondered whether she'd done the right thing telling them about their suspicions about Patsy. 'But Dad, Lex and I don't know for sure if Patsy instigated the whole thing.'

Bernie shook his head. 'I know, love, but it makes sense now you've told us all that.' He sighed as if he were in pain. 'What really is a mystery though, is why she would do something so mean at all?'

'If she did,' Gwen threw Susie a glance, 'then she's done a terrible thing.'

Susie groaned. 'That's exactly what Lex said, but I'm so mixed up about it all, Mum. One moment I think we've got it all wrong, the next I'm convinced she did instigate it. Part of me wants to believe she's innocent, yet another part can't help thinking she isn't. I feel her letter to Gloria is very revealing regarding her intentions.'

'It's possible Patsy is concerned about Lex two-timing someone she sees as a friend,' Gwen ventured, one eyebrow raised.

'Maybe, Mum — but why lie? If she felt it was something she ought to intervene in, why not just write and say that he's seeing me again?'

Gwen shook her head. 'I really don't know.'

'Then there's this evening's incident of her being found in the stream.'

'I simply don't believe she tried to harm herself — she must know how shallow that stream is. Maybe she was distraught and fell and became stuck, or momentarily blacked out or something?'

Despair gnawed at Susie.

Supposing Patsy really had tried to harm herself — what's more, supposing she'd succeeded? Her heart contracted at Patsy's pain. What happened to the girl two years ago to cause her to change from a sweet friend to a scheming enemy?

'I think I ought to go round there and have a talk with Beattie and Len,' Bernie proposed.

That horrible feeling still gnawed at Susie's insides. 'No, Dad, please.'

She turned to her mum and said, 'Tell him he mustn't do or say anything yet. Not until we know for sure — and until we know how Patsy is.'

Gwen pulled a face.

'I can't influence your dad that much, love. If Bernie is set on something then that's it.'

She turned and looked directly at Bernie.

'However, Susie has a point. You can't go blundering in there making accusations about Patsy, it wouldn't be right.'

'Especially now,' Susie put in quickly, 'now that Patsy's had an accident.'

Susie could see her dad was mulling it over.

'In that case . . . '

He shrugged, shook his head and sighed like a man who'd just lost a battle.

'I'll wait until there's obvious evidence that Patsy is to blame for the fall-out between our families. Mind you — ' He looked intently at them both. 'I shall act on the smallest bit of evidence. Do you understand?'

Susie's stomach knotted again. Her dad was seriously cross and she couldn't blame him for that. If Patsy was responsible for the big fall-out between their families, then the trouble she caused could still have far-reaching effects.

She gritted her teeth — like Gloria, for a start!

The phone in the hall rang and all three of them jumped up.

Susie was at the door first. 'It'll be Lex!'

'No.' Bernie eased past. 'I'll get it.'

He picked up the phone receiver. 'Yes, it is . . . All right, thank you, I'll let her know immediately.'

He put the receiver down and turned to Susie. 'It was your evening class person — the class will be this Tuesday evening instead of Wednesday, the normal place and time. They said to let them know if you can't make it.'

'Oh.' Susie was disappointed it wasn't Lex, but glad she knew about the change of day for her evening class, for somehow just the mention of the class empowered her. 'I'm not sure I can make it, though.'

'Of course you can, love. You can leave the shop earlier on Tuesday. I'll put a casserole on low in the oven at lunch time and you can eat before you leave.'

'All right — but keep things as they usually are and I'll have a burger in town afterwards.'

Just thinking of the burger bar sent several sensations pitching through Susie.

So much had happened the previous afternoon, so many mind-blowing revelations, so many mixed emotions, so many astonishing surprises and revelations!

She thought of the students. When everything was sorted out she would ring Sally — although whether her fledgling idea was viable or not was another matter.

'Don't worry, Mum.' She leaned over and gave her mum a peck on the cheek. 'I won't starve.'

With that settled, they trooped back to the sitting room. No sooner had they sat down when the phone rang again. Again, they all jumped.

'I'll get it!' Susie was at the door first again.

Although Bernie was beside her, he agreed and lightly inclined his head to Gwen. 'It could be the class re-arranging again.'

Gwen sidled past them. 'It could be for me,' she announced firmly. 'You know some people like to order groceries on a Sunday evening so they're ready for Monday mornings.'

She had a point. Bernie threw Susie a

look and Susie and her dad hung back to let Gwen answer the phone — but they both followed her.

'Gwen Cotting here . . . oh hello, yes . . . ' As Susie put her hand out to take the receiver, Gwen shook her head.

There was silence as they listened.

'Who is it?' Susie mouthed.

'Lex,' Gwen mouthed back.

'Yes, thank you so much for letting us know Lex . . . we're very grateful . . . I'll pass on the news.'

She put the receiver down with a slow silent deliberate movement.

'Patsy's all right but a bit confused. She's talked to the police and was put straight into bed with lots of hot water bottles afterwards. The doctor visited and gave her some medication to help her sleep.'

'Did Lex say why she was in the stream?'

'No. It appears that after Lex went off with her letter she went for a walk under the railway bridge by the stream and says she can't remember anything after that until someone pulled her out of the water. Everyone in the family is taking it in turns to sit by her bed during the night.'

Susie looked at her parents.

'I think we could all do with a hot milky drink then a bit of an early night,' she suggested.

Once in the kitchen Susie saw the unused tea tray. Her thoughts were bitter-sweet. Even the rosé wine was mainly untouched.

That night though, the hideous dreams twisted through her sleep all night long. Even as she dreamed, Susie knew that somewhere deep in those dreams was a clue to everything; a revolting clue hiding beneath a jagged briar of menace.

★   ★   ★

The removal van arrived as Susie was helping Mr Rowe down the front stairs.

'I'm going to miss you all,' Mrs Rowe

said from behind them, 'but it's for the best.'

Susie swallowed. 'We'll miss you too but remember, I'll be visiting you very soon.'

'We don't know what we'd have done without all your help yesterday. The removal men only have to take the main furniture, load the boxes and they're done.'

Susie managed a half smile. This would be much more of an emotional blow if it was all she was thinking of, but her bad dreams whirred in her head. She couldn't always remember them but she still knew they were dark, nerve-racking, with a scarily imminent feeling. Dashing the scary dreams from her mind, she forced a half-smile.

Mrs Shottle, as tactlessly direct as she was, had a kind heart and had organised a little farewell do.

'The whole street will be out to see you off.'

Mr Rowe shuffled onto the last stair.

'Glad to see the back of us no doubt,' he chortled.

'Not at all,' Susie reassured him. 'You've both been pillars of this community since you arrived.'

The old man smiled. 'I'll be sad to leave, that's for sure — but I'll also be glad not to have any stairs.'

Susie nodded. That's what Lex had said.

Although the Rowes knew the neighbours would be there to wave them off, she didn't tell them that her mum was going to close the shop for twenty minutes or so while they supplied tea and home made cakes as a little farewell do. That was to be a surprise. It wasn't really long enough but as the Rowes needed to be at their bungalow when the removal van got there, it was all the time they had.

'Are you ready for the off?' Gwen asked as Susie led them into the shop.

'Just about,' Mrs Rowe gulped.

Gwen swallowed back her emotion. 'I've already ordered your taxi to coincide with the removal van leaving.'

Susie glanced out of the window, and observed, 'And here comes Mrs Shottle and the others laden with goodies.'

Soon the little farewell party was under way with Mr and Mrs Rowe sitting in prime position in the middle of the shop chatting about their memories with almost everyone in the street who had come to see them off.

When at last a large black taxi drew up, the women lapsed into silence as Mr and Mrs Rowe made their way out of the shop.

'Thank you all so much,' Mrs Rowe sniffed when they were on the pavement. 'I had no idea we were going to have this kind farewell.'

She looked at Gwen and choking back tears added, 'I shall miss you so much, dear Gwen.'

The taxi driver was already opening the door when suddenly there was a horrible yell from along the street.

'Oi, you!' The air stilled as everyone looked in the direction of the shout.

'Which one of you owns that shop on that corner?'

As the man lumbering towards them in florid rage reached the group on the pavement, they parted to let him through.

Ignoring all that was going on he addressed everyone. 'Which one of you silly — ' Susie realised he was about to use foul language but seeing the mass of astonished women obviously thought better of it. 'Which idiot filled my stupid son's head with ideas of working at window cleaning?'

He swivelled and seemed to snarl, his mouth was so contorted with fury. 'Come on then, which one of you had the ridiculous notion that my son was fit for such work?'

Gwen pushed to the fore.

'He cleaned the shop windows and when the suggestion was made that he could clean others too, we followed it through by offering him ladders and any equipment he might need.'

As the man rounded on Gwen several

women took it upon themselves to form a protective semi-circle about her.

Although the man took a pace back, he was still enraged. 'Do you know what you've done, you interfering old woman?'

Mrs Shottle forced herself between him and Gwen. 'How dare you speak to a member of our community like that! Someone, I might add, who is the very core of what we all stand for here in Willbob Street!'

The man threw back his head and with a mocking laugh turned on Mrs Shottle.

'Ha, the very core you say? The very upright core of this community, is she? Well.' His mouth curled, his nostrils flared and his already red face darkened to crimson. 'Your very upright core of the community has encouraged my lazy, layabout son to get ideas above his station, and when I refused to allow him to do as you suggested, do you know what he did? Do you?'

Before anyone managed to speak he

hurried on, 'I'll tell you what he did! He began breaking into shops and wrecking and stealing things from them.' He turned to Gwen again and banged his hand against his head. 'Worse than that, it turns out he had something to do with an incident at a stream near here! You and your interfering turned his brain to even more nastiness!'

Gwen huffed in a breath. 'More nastiness? Roy hasn't got a nasty bone in his body.'

'Get out of here before I call the police!' Mrs Shottle was well and truly riled. 'If your son is the shop raider it has nothing to do with Mrs Cotting. All she tried to do was help him.'

'Call the police?' he sneered. 'I can assure you the police have already been called. Where do you think I've been all morning? The police station, that's where! You think I've nothing better to do than answer questions about what that lazy good-for-nothing does and where he goes? You think I haven't got a proper job to go to?'

He turned to thrust his way out through the crowd of women that now seemed to have swelled to a larger group even than those attending the farewell party. 'You haven't heard the last of this, believe you me!'

His robust exit left a stillness behind.

Susie wished Lex had been able to come — he would have known how to handle Roy's father — but his family needed him more.

Gwen stared mutely at Susie.

Placing a gentle guiding arm round her, Susie said, 'Let's just concentrate on saying goodbye to Mr and Mrs Rowe, shall we?'

When the taxi and removal van rolled away, the farewells were subdued as the vehicles disappeared from Willbob Street.

Susie swallowed back the lump in her throat.

Roy was the shop raider? She could hardly believe it! He seemed so gentle and shy. How could she have got him so wrong? Had he turned up out of the blue so he could get some idea of the layout of their shop?

'I'll open up now.' Gwen broke the silence.

Susie was angry as well as confused by what had just happened. All she wanted to do was tell all the nosy, lingering women that the show was over and would they all just go away!

True as that was, she realised it wouldn't help the situation — nor would it be conducive to good customer relations.

So all she said was, 'I'm going to help Mum now, please come in and collect your things when you're ready. Thank you all for your support.'

With that she followed her Gwen into the shop.

When Mrs Shottle followed them in before anyone else, Susie was on her guard. Irrespective of the way she had stood up for Gwen, Susie felt that Mrs Shottle might have something negative to say about Roy.

'Ladies,' Susie announced before Mrs

Shottle could get a word in. 'Please feel free to stay and shop just as usual.'

She turned to their opinionated customer. 'Thank you so much for your support just now, Mrs Shottle.'

'It was nothing,' Mrs Shottle coughed. 'But I certainly don't believe that Roy is the guilty party.'

She turned to the others and announced, 'I don't believe a word of it — nor do I believe the rumours about him being light-fingered either. Having now seen his father I think the lad's problems are due to the father's attitude. Having witnessed him first-hand, I'm surprised young Roy is so willing to please at all! As far as I'm concerned he can come and clean my windows any time whenever he's available.' She took Susie and Gwen in with one intense look. 'And I think it would be good if your family were to offer him the flat!'

Susie gasped. 'We'll do no such thing!'

'Your loss.' Mrs Shottle put down a

tray of empty cups and plates and a second later the door-bell tinkled as she stalked out.

'Don't mind her, love,' Gwen smiled. 'She means well, and she did me proud the way she saw Roy's dad off.'

There was a murmur of approval and Susie nodded but kept her thoughts to herself.

★　★　★

By lunchtime everything seemed to be back to normal, but Susie knew her mum was still upset.

'I thought Lex might pop in,' Gwen mused checking the cakes in chilled counter cabinet.

Susie's heart skipped a beat.

'Me too.' She glanced at the shop clock. 'I doubt he'll come now, though.'

What she tried to avoid thinking about was that, although the onlookers might not know what Roy's dad meant, Susie was aware that 'an incident at the nearby stream' meant Roy could have been involved in Patsy's accident. If so, would Lex think they were to blame for encouraging Roy?

Susie's stomach churned.

13

As it happened, Lex didn't arrive until mid-afternoon — and when he did, he asked to see Susie alone.

'You can talk in front of Mum. I've told her everything,' Susie insisted.

'In that case . . . ' He looked at Gwen who was slicing ham ready for a regular order. 'I can start by telling you that there's been an arrest.'

Gwen stopped slicing to look up at Lex. 'We've heard,' she told him.

Lex looked uncomfortable. 'You have?'

'Yes — and who.' Gwen resumed slicing.

Lex looked from Gwen to Susie. 'When did the police come here?'

Susie's brow creased. 'Police? Why would the police come and tell us?'

Lex's hair, usually so immaculate and tidy, appeared to be ruffled and wayward and as he ran his fingers through it. He looked at them in confusion. 'Because of the *Hetty's* bag that was found near the stream where Patsy was?'

Shaking her head in disbelief, Susie could hardly breathe. 'We haven't seen the police. We didn't know about the *Hetty's* bag.'

Lex placed his hands flat on the counter. 'Did you know that a *Hetty's* bag has been found in all the ransacked shops?'

Gwen gulped and stopped slicing.

'All of them?'

Her hand shook as she tore a bag off the strip on the end of the counter ready for the ham.

Lex gave a deep sigh. 'I must say I'm surprised to hear that Roy Sawson is implicated, but as that was the only name Patsy remembered when questioned about the incident, the police had to act quickly.'

Susie looked at him in confusion and opened her mouth to speak, but whatever it was she was going to say was cut short with the tinkling of the doorbell as a policeman entered the shop.

Taking off his helmet, he addressed Gwen.

'I'm sorry to impose at this time of day — ' He turned as the door-bell tinkled again when two women came in.

Susie suspected they had seen the constable in the street, watched where he went and decided to see what was going on. They probably wouldn't even think they were being nosy, just looking out for each other and doing folk a service by passing information round.

Why was she being so cynical? There was something in her mind, something important and relevant — but it vanished with the appearance of the constable.

'I've just sliced the ham you ordered,' Gwen beamed — rather too cheerfully — to one of the women who had just come in.

Feeling ashamed at her uncharitable thoughts, yet still confused, Susie just about managed a wry smile.

The women lingered rather too long, and the police constable stayed silent.

Eventually Lex took charge. 'Do you wish to see anyone in particular, sir?'

The constable nodded. 'The proprietor.' He glanced at Gwen and then at Susie. 'And Miss Cotting, if I may. If that's convenient?'

Lex nodded. 'In that case, I'll man the shop while you're away.'

With that, he turned to the two women and with an engaging smile asked, 'Is there anything else I can get for you, ladies?'

Supressing a smile at the way Lex took command of the awkward situation, Susie followed her mum and the constable into the shop kitchen.

★   ★   ★

'Goodness, that was intense.' Gwen shuddered once back out on the shop floor again.

Susie knew exactly how her mum felt.

'I still can't believe it,' she said.

'I know.' Gwen's voice dropped as she added, 'But I don't think he should have told us that Roy's dad said Roy was so out of control that he should be sent to the Borstal, do you?'

Susie winced. Why would any parent do that? 'He never struck me as being out of control.'

'There you are, madam,' Lex beamed, putting a *Hetty's* brown paper bag next to the others on the counter.

After the customer left, Lex turned to them.

'You both look as if you've had a shock. Why don't you go home for the rest of the afternoon? I can manage here.'

'Certainly not,' Gwen puffed. 'I'm perfectly fine.' She glanced at Susie. 'I think it hit you harder, love . . . why don't you go home?'

'I'm quite all right,' Susie snapped.

'That's a relief,' Lex declared, 'I was rather worried about you.'

Swallowing back a tight feeling in her throat, Susie retorted, 'I'm perfectly capable of handling bad news, Lex.'

She said it in a way that made him want to kiss all her unhappiness away.

However all he said, was, 'I was thinking that I'd like to see that new comedy play in Wynnton tonight. What about you?'

In spite of her despondency, Susie's spirits lifted at his conciliatory tone.

'It had good reviews in the local paper, but I doubt I'd be very good company tonight.'

'I think a comedy would do you some good, love.' Gwen smiled.

'Gwen's right, darling.'

As Lex's gentle gaze trickled over her, Susie's knees went weak, and her spine felt feathery as those tiny diamond-clad ballerinas started warming up for their nerve-tingling pirouetting. In spite of her misery about Roy and Patsy, she knew she was blushing with an absurd pleasure.

'In that case, I would love to go.'

Lex's face lit up, and until then, she hadn't realised how grave his expression had been.

'It starts at seven-thirty, so I'll pick you up in time to catch the six-thirty bus and we could grab a coffee in the new burger bar beforehand — if that's all right with you?'

Coffee in a burger bar didn't seem right when Roy was locked up somewhere for something Susie was sure he didn't do.

But to refuse would also mean explaining why she felt he was innocent . . .

★ ★ ★

Having taken extra care to look her best, Susie stepped out of the front

260

door in her dolly mixture blue coat at precisely twenty past six.

'You look gorgeous, darling,' Lex beamed when he saw her. 'Of course you always look gorgeous, but that coat matches your eyes perfectly.'

Knowing she was blushing, Susie glanced slightly to one side — and in doing so caught the briefest glimpse of someone dodging out of sight round the corner opposite the shop. Was someone spying on their shop?

Suppressing a shudder she smiled up at Lex.

His brow rose. 'Is everything all right?'

Susie swallowed. Why had he asked that?

'Yes, why?'

Tucking her hand and arm into his elbow, Lex shrugged. 'I don't know really. You just looked a bit . . . well, off.'

'Just a déjà vu moment, I think.'

Lex grinned. 'Well, we've done this before haven't we?'

'Many times.' She squeezed his elbow with her arm, and consigning her silly suspicions to an impenetrable part of her brain, changed the subject. 'How's Patsy doing?'

'She's assured us that whatever happened it wasn't anything she did on purpose. She's determined to go to work and forget about it.' He let out a sigh. 'I can't help wondering if she's hiding something, though. Perhaps her moodiness and angry outbursts point to something going on, something she can't talk about.'

'Have you tried asking her?'

'I don't think she's fit enough at the moment.'

Susie's heart filled with compassion for Patsy. If only they could put the past behind them and become friends again.

★   ★   ★

Much later that evening when they reached the back gate of Susie's house, Lex paused.

'Oh darling,' he whispered drawing her towards him. 'This brings back so many wonderful memories of holding you close. I love you so much. Nothing will ever part us again.'

Suddenly Susie felt ensnared and caught up in a situation she couldn't control! She pushed him away so hard that when he reeled backwards, he almost tripped on the cobbles.

Obviously shocked, Lex regained his balance and stared at her. 'Susie, you're trembling.'

'I'm not.'

It was only when Lex put his arms round her and pulled her close to him again that she knew he was right. She was trembling so hard she could hardly stand.

'Darling, what is it? What's wrong?'

'I don't know,' Susie whispered. 'I can't really explain it. I think this alleyway gives me the creeps, that's all.'

Lex tenderly escorted her to the back door and into the kitchen.

'I'll just say goodnight to your

parents then I'll be off, sweetheart,' he said after turning on the light.

He didn't attempt to kiss her again and although it was her own silly fault, Susie felt deprived. She had behaved in an irrational way reacting to his embrace like that! What on earth came over her?

Yet somewhere inside, she still shuddered.

* * *

When Lex came into the shop early the following morning asking to see her alone, Susie was embarrassed all over again. She felt sure he would quiz her about the previous night.

Once they were outside and walking however, he took her hand. 'I have something to ask you.'

'I know, and I am so sorry Lex,' she blurted.

Lex swivelled to face her. 'You're sorry?' He shook his head. 'I thought we had turned so many corners, Susie.

264

Is it something I've done — or not done? Something said . . . ?'

'It has nothing to do with you at all Lex. It happened so suddenly . . . '

He looked into her face and swallowed hard. 'I thought you wanted this as much as I do.' Susie stared at him in dismay. He looked so wretched she didn't know what to say. 'I should have waited until all this mess with Patsy and Gloria is cleared up. But can we still go on seeing each other until I go off to North Coates at least?'

Susie's jaw dropped and her stomach churned. Could this be happening all over again?

'I thought you loved me? I thought you meant it when you asked me to marry you.'

'Susie.' He took her hands in his. 'When I just said that I have something to ask you, your immediate response was that you knew but you were sorry. Where did I go wrong?'

'I thought you were asking me about last night, that's why I said I was sorry.'

Suddenly she giggled — so many misunderstandings! 'I'm sorry about last night, I don't know what came over me.'

'We're talking at cross-purposes, so I'll start again.' He cleared his throat and right there in the street put her hands to his lips. 'I wanted it to be more romantic, but my darling Susie, will you marry me as soon as I can get a licence, rather than waiting any longer? I mean before I go to North Coates. We could get a special licence — it'll only take three weeks.'

Susie's heart skipped several beats! He was right — nothing would ever tear them apart again!

Lex put his lips close to her ear, and dropping his voice to a sultry sensual murmur, he whispered, 'We could even have a two-week honeymoon.'

Although his breath came out in wisps as soft as fluffy thistledown, the velvet sumptuousness of his tone caused her spine to instantly begin shimmying with those diamond-spangled dancers now dancing on luxurious voluptuous cushions!

In three weeks she could be Lex's wife? Only three weeks? It made her brain frothy, her knees wobble, and somewhere deep within, the heat of longing slid within her.

'Yes! Oh, Lex, let's do it!'

She didn't have time to say any more because a second later he was kissing her into wonderful oblivion! She felt light! She felt heavy! She felt dizzy! She longed for more!

When a last he drew away from her, she felt oddly deprived, yet the silky warmth permeating through her made her feel as if she was floating on a cushion of balmy air.

'I love you so much, Susie. I want us to be together forever — as soon as possible.'

'Yes, forever,' she whispered before, not heeding or hearing the disapproving tutting of passers-by, they kissed again.

★ ★ ★

Putting on her wind-jammer, Susie went into the back living-room.

'I'll be off in a moment,' she said.

Gwen looked up from her recipe book.

'You're still going to your class even though there's so much to do?'

Susie's heart gave an excited skitter. She had considered missing it, but instead she said, 'Yes, because it may be my last one as the spring term ends next week — and when the term restarts, I'll be with Lex.'

Her insides fizzed with excitement and pleasure. They'd begun the process of sorting out the wedding licence almost immediately, the date was set, and everything was now in motion.

She'd even started designing the perfect dress in her head — a simple fitted shift.

'Besides, Dad told them that I'd definitely be there tonight.'

'It might be nice if you made up the floral bouquets for your wedding, love.'

Bernie peeked up over his paper,

caught Susie's eye and winked. 'I think she needs more space than we have here for that, Gwen. Flowers all over the place always set you off sneezing and you wouldn't want to be red-eyed for our daughter's big day would you?'

Gwen placed her finger on a picture of a beautiful wedding cake. 'I would not,' she chuckled then added more seriously, 'What about this?'

Susie glanced at the cake. To her, it wasn't about cake or dresses or bridesmaids or spending vast amounts of money — it was being Mrs Lex Maceul that really mattered!

Bernie gave Susie a tender smile. 'You'd better be on your way if you want to catch the twenty past six bus, love.'

★   ★   ★

'Are you waiting for someone ducks?'

Swinging round Susie saw the caretaker of the hall the class met in each Wednesday. 'Yes, my class was changed from Wednesday to Tuesday but there's usually someone here by now.'

The caretaker shrugged sympathetically. 'The Tuesday class was cancelled too. Apparently only one person could make it tonight.'

'I told them I could make it.'

'That must be you, then. I'm the only one here. If I were you, I'd go and get a cup of tea from that new burger bar you young folks like, and then go off home.'

'Yes — then at least it won't be a completely wasted journey, will it?'

Perhaps Sally and her friends from the design school would be there again.

★   ★   ★

Ten minutes later she was ordering a coffee.

'Sorry about the juke box,' the owner grinned sheepishly. 'There's someone coming in tomorrow to fix it.'

Thanking him for her tea, Susie smiled. 'That's all right I like the quiet. I'll people-watch instead.'

The owner looked around. 'Not many people in tonight though.' He glanced across to the door as two young women about Susie's age entered. 'I'll direct them to the next table to you,' he grinned. 'Then you can people-watch all you want.'

Susie smiled. It was only when the two young women sat down at the next table that she realised she recognised one of them.

Gloria!

Her stomach instantly churned and knotted. No, it couldn't be! Why was she here? Had Patsy managed to get a message to her after all?

Then her heart bounced with anticipation. Maybe Lex got in touch with her and asked to see her face to face?

Susie heard Gloria's companion speak.

'Are you sure you're going the right way about this?' she asked.

'What else can I do?' Gloria snapped.

'You're sure he loves you? Enough to marry you?' her companion pressed.

Marry? Susie nearly collapsed!

'Of course I'm sure! Patsy is always saying how much Lex adores me. Every time she writes she says that Lex doesn't show his feelings, but she knows that he's madly in love with me.'

'But a baby, Gloria . . . how will he feel about you being pregnant?'

Susie almost spat out her drink in shock! Gloria was pregnant? She didn't want to hear any more — yet she couldn't tear herself away! She was sinking in a haze of shock and pain.

'When I tell him I'm pregnant he'll fall to his knees and beg me to marry him!'

'But Gloria . . . '

Suddenly Susie's haze evaporated, and with a composure she didn't feel, she inched from her seat and walked calmly from the burger bar. Once outside she ran to the bus stop, dashing the tears from her eyes as she went.

The conversation in the burger bar continued without her there to hear it . . .

'But Gloria nothing!' Gloria's Hollywood blonde waves bounced. 'You're always telling me what a catch I am, Linda. Besides lots of men do it, whether they know it or not, they take on another man's child.'

'What if he meets another woman? I just can't believe you began seeing that married man again, Gloria — and while dating Lex!'

'I couldn't help myself,' Gloria wailed.

'For someone who never wanted children I'm surprised you weren't more careful.'

'You know it was being the eldest of seven that made me feel like that. The MOD typing pool was my escape from all that.'

'Not now,' Linda returned wryly. 'Now marriage is your escape. It's a shame Lex was always a perfect gentleman — otherwise you could actually pretend the baby was his.'

'Do you think I don't know that?' Gloria growled in frustration.

It was still light when Susie reached home and she crept round the back through the kitchen, hoping to tiptoe past the back sitting room and go straight upstairs without anyone seeing the state she was in.

It was bad enough waiting for the bus and having to stifle her sobs by blowing her nose then burying her face in her handkerchief as her mind repeated over and over again, *Lex is going to be a father!*

'Hello, love.' Gwen was just drying up two cups as Susie entered the kitchen. 'You're early.'

Trying not to sound as if there was anything wrong, Susie said, 'The class was cancelled.'

Gwen glanced at the kitchen clock. 'In that case, you're late.' She scanned Susie's face with concern. 'Susie, are you all right?'

Knots of jagged barbed wire stuck in Susie's throat and all she could do was nod. She must not give in to tears now! She had to hold it all back until she was safely under her eiderdown where her parents wouldn't hear her despairing sobs — sobs that threatened to burst out in an uncontrollable torrent of heartbreak any second.

If that happened then she would have to explain, and she wasn't ready to go through all she'd heard in the burger bar yet.

Gwen frowned. 'I think you may be coming down with something. Go on up to bed and I'll bring up a cup of hot lemon and honey.'

Knowing her current state had nothing to do with anything except agonising grief, Susie shook her head.

'I'll be all right,' she croaked.

'Nonsense, lemon and honey will do you good. Now off you go.'

Feeling a fraud Susie nodded. Her mum thinking she had a cold would give her more time to prepare for the terrible bombshell that Lex would very soon dropping on them all.

As she went upstairs all she could think of was that Gloria was pregnant and that Lex was going to be a father!

14

Forcing the last drop of honey and lemon down, Susie sniffed and attempted to clear what felt like parched stones blocking her throat.

'Thanks,' she rasped. 'I'm sure I'll be better in the morning.'

Better in the morning? Susie slid down into the covers. She'd never be better again!

'Just rest.' Gwen pulled the covers right up to Susie's chin. 'We can't have you being ill in the run-up to your wedding, can we?'

A swell of tears instantly gathered somewhere behind her nose. Susie could hardly breathe let alone speak.

'Doe — ' she mumbled, then with a supreme valiant effort added, 'Don't talk of weddings.'

'I understand,' Gwen murmured soothingly.

Bernie popped his head round the bedroom door. 'I think this hot toddy will do you the world of good, love.'

Susie didn't want hot toddy. She wanted to be left alone to grieve. She wanted to nurse her wounded soul in her own way by sobbing without interruption in the darkness only her bedcovers could provide.

'She's just had honey and lemon.'

'In that case this is the perfect addition.'

As Susie sipped the hot toddy the liquid relaxed her aching throat and a gentle calm seeped softly through her.

'There,' her dad's voice seemed a long way off. 'That's done you good already. You'll sleep well tonight.'

Somewhere from the back of her mind Susie knew she didn't want to sleep. She wanted to cry all night until she had no tears left. Too emotionally drained and too mentally exhausted with the effort of holding back her emotions however, she drifted into sleep.

★ ★ ★

In the early hours, Gloria's conversation invaded Susie's dreams like a disagreeable interloper and caused her to wake with a start.

Her first reaction was utter relief that it was a horrible nightmare and that Gloria wasn't pregnant after all — then as she went through it in her mind, the conversation in the burger bar came back in a horrendous rush.

It wasn't a dream! Gloria was pregnant and expected Lex to marry her!

How could she have been such a fool not to realise that Lex and Gloria's relationship was so serious? How could she have missed the signs?

Lex! her mind wailed. *How could you? How could you say you love me and want to marry me when all the time Gloria was pregnant? How could you lead me on? How could you be so thoughtless and cruel?*

Her thoughts tumbled on — supposing Gloria hadn't turned up and she

279

and Lex married and *then* they discovered Gloria was pregnant? It didn't bear thinking about!

Of course Lex would now do the decent thing and marry Gloria — he would not abandon the mother of his child. It wasn't in his nature to be cowardly and irresponsible.

Thorns of grief and despair pierced Susie's insides. Lex *had* behaved irresponsibly though — and cowardly too, because despite his intimate relationship with Gloria he was prepared to ditch her without a thought!

Oh, Lex, how could you?

Susie slid under the bedcovers and sobbed.

★　★　★

Bernie put his head round the bedroom door. 'Not feeling better, I hear?'

Although Susie had sobbed for hours, she eventually fell asleep again and only woke up when her mum arrived with a morning cup of tea.

Gwen frowned sympathetically. 'I do hope you've only got a summer cold. Hopefully this tea will help clear up that blocked feeling?'

Susie knew nothing would help, but took the tea anyway. Feeling guilty at her mum's anxiety and unnecessary fretting, but still grief-stricken, puffy-eyed and sniffing, Susie could only shake her aching head and silently sip the tea.

'I think I'll call the doctor.'

Bernie stepped into the bedroom and up to the bed. 'Have you got a temperature, love?'

Gwen answered for her. 'No, she hasn't. I checked while she was still sleeping; her forehead is quite cool.'

'In that case, leave it for today and if she isn't better tomorrow then we'll get the doctor round. A day in bed should help.'

Susie was faintly bemused yet mildly put out that they thought she was too ill to think for herself. 'I don't need a doctor,' she mumbled.

Gwen plumped Susie's pillows. 'In that case, I'll bring up some cold-cure powder.'

Susie knew nothing would ease the pain she was feeling. No amount of cold-cure powder, no amount of tea, and no amount of concerned care would take away her heartbreak. All she wanted was to be left alone.

Susie was relieved when her dad went off to work and her mum eventually went to open the shop. At last now she could cry as much as she needed to without anyone hearing.

⋆ ⋆ ⋆

Reading the hand delivered note again, Lex banged on Patsy's door.

'I need to speak to you Patsy. Let me in!'

'I'm getting ready for work.'

Lex knew how determined Patsy was to get back to normal, although he wasn't sure what her normality was any more.

'Are you decent?'

At that moment Patsy threw open her door. 'Of course I'm decent, I have to leave in a minute!'

Lex held the letter up. 'Has this got anything to do with you?'

Patsy drew back. 'What is it?'

Lex waved the letter in front of her. 'It must have arrived either late last night or early this morning. It was hand delivered.'

Patsy pulled a face. 'Why should I know anything about a hand-delivered letter? Who's it from anyway?'

Not wanting to put Patsy on the defensive, Lex moderated his tone. 'It appears to be from Gloria asking me to meet her in that new burger bar in town today at ten.'

Patsy frowned. 'I can assure you it has nothing to do with me.' However, her face paled slightly as she glanced at the letter but her tone remained neutral. 'Why would Gloria deliver a letter? Why not just knock on the door and ask to see you?'

'That's exactly my question, Patsy.' His words hung in the air as he waited for an explanation. None came. 'Have you contacted her?'

A muscle in her jaw twitched and Lex sensed she was flustered. 'No. My last letter to her was on Sunday, which as far as I know wasn't posted. Unless you changed the address and posted it?'

Studying her closely, Lex aimed for slow deliberation. 'I suspect you already know the answer to that, Patsy.'

'Am I to understand you opened a letter not addressed to you?' she demanded shrilly.

'Yes.' Lex purposely kept his voice soft. 'And as you can imagine I was shocked at the content.'

The muscles in Patsy's jaw twitched and her face hardened. 'You had no right! May I remind you it's against the law to open correspondence that isn't addressed to you?'

Lex drew a deep calculating breath then let it go very slowly. 'And I'm sure *you* know that interfering in mail by opening or discarding it is a criminal offence, too — especially,' he continued carefully, 'if one is in a position of great trust through one's job.'

Patsy's eyes narrowed. 'Get out of my way, Lex — or I'll be late.' Brushing past him, she rushed down the stairs.

Lex leaned over the stair rail and called after her, 'We aren't going to expose you, Patsy!'

Coming to an abrupt halt, Patsy swung round to look back up at him.

'Expose me? You really have no idea what you've done!'

With that, she raced out of the front door.

This time, Lex didn't go after her. Putting Patsy into a panic wasn't his intention, but right now he had other things on his mind.

Why had Gloria left him a note in such a strange manner? Could he even be sure it *was* from Gloria? Now he was being daft! If it wasn't Gloria, who else would have left it?

'Everyone hopes you get well soon.' Gwen handed Susie a mug of chicken soup.

Although still blocked up because she'd cried herself to sleep again, Susie's hiccupping sobs had subsided, for the more she thought about Lex, the more she realised she had to let him go graciously. She had no right to hold him back.

Besides, Gloria was the one who'd sold herself short to a man who didn't love her! And even though that hurt, the circumstances and Gloria's condition would not change.

Susie had to be strong. She was going to be the better person. She would let him go gracefully however much it hurt!

In spite of her valiant resolutions, however, she wasn't sure her throat would function properly.

'I can't, Mum.'

'Just have a sip — it'll do you good.'

Knowing her mum needed to go back to the shop to do a Wednesday afternoon stock-take and not wanting to delay her, Susie obediently took the mug and sipped. Having the soup meant there wouldn't be much chatting, because although she would have to tell her parents about Gloria, she didn't want to go through it just yet.

'I thought Lex might come into the shop,' Gwen mused. 'If he does, should I send him up to see you?'

Susie almost choked. 'No,' she spluttered.

'I understand you don't want him to see you like this love, but remember you'll be spending the rest of your life with him and — '

Susie thrust the cup at her mum. 'No!'

In spite of her decision to let Lex go gracefully, Susie's mind had veered from anguish at not being able to spend the rest of her life with him to plotting her future without him.

Of course she could manage without

him. She could be a career girl now, and she would contact Sally with her brilliant idea! Once Mum and Dad were over the shock of Lex having to marry Gloria, they'd be thrilled with what she had planned.

It went through her head again as she outlined and replayed it all once more.

She would ask Sally and the others to design and make an up-to-the-minute clothing collection. The collection could be stored in the flat above the shop, and then shown through the Party Plan method. It might take some work regarding promotion and advertising but as Sally had mentioned sisters and friends, invitations to the events could be extended to them as well. Susie could also place cards in shop windows announcing the events.

Naturally there would have to be some changes in the flat. A new carpet and some chairs and other furniture in the living-room area, a tweak to the double bedroom to become a dressing room with storage. Plus — but she wasn't quite so sure of this part yet — a bit of an update in the kitchen to incorporate one of those new-fangled washing machines that did everything.

Oh — she could see it all in her mind!

Already she was reaching an acceptance that only a few hours ago she had thought was beyond her capabilities.

She didn't need Lex! She would contact Sally with her idea this afternoon and get things in motion straight away!

Waiting until she heard Mum go into the shop, Susie went to the drawer where she had put the piece of paper with Sally's number on. Looking at it for a moment made her feel she was on a precipice of change, and with a sense of renewed purpose she went downstairs to the telephone.

★   ★   ★

'Yes, thank you, and as I mentioned, I don't want her to leave a message with anyone. Please ask her to ask for me in person.'

Susie solemnly replaced the receiver. She should have realised Sally would be in school, but had she done the right thing? Of course she had!

Padding into the kitchen she looked at the clock. It was after two.

Gloria would have told him by now! Irrespective of all her resolutions, her stomach churned and her head swirled with renewed chaotic turmoil! How would Lex react when Gloria announced she was pregnant? What would he say? How soon would they get married?

That barbed wire lodged in her throat again.

Getting a glass out of the cupboard, she filled it with water. Then with immense willpower, she shoved all her turbulence aside, raised the glass in the air, and called out, 'To my new life!'

Just as the echo of her voice died down, the telephone rang. Susie stilled.

It could only be Lex! Anger suddenly blazed through her. Did he not have the guts to tell her face to face?

Bolting to the telephone, she whisked up the receiver. 'Yes!'

There was a pause then a very polite voice said, 'Mum said you rang.'

'Sally?'

'Yes.'

'Sally — I've had a brilliant idea!'

Sally was so thrilled with Susie's plans that by the time they finished talking, it was all worked out. Sally would set things going at her end, and Susie would start preparing the flat.

Now all she had to do was tell her parents everything . . .

★ ★ ★

'It's good to see you up, love, even if . . .'

Susie blinked up from the sofa. After her conversation with Sally, Susie went into the sitting room to continue planning how, but regardless of her enthusiasm, she fell asleep.

'I came down for a drink of water

291

then came in here ... I must have dozed off.'

Gwen hesitated and something inside Susie juddered. Had Lex been into the shop and confessed all? 'What?'

Gwen sat down next to Susie. 'Roy came into the shop today. He hasn't been charged with any crime,' Gwen told her. 'His name was mentioned by Patsy because she and Roy are dating.'

Susie gasped. 'Roy and Patsy — dating?'

'Yes, it was Patsy who told Roy to come to us.'

Susie struggled to take it in. It wasn't Patsy seeing Roy that perplexed her; it was that Patsy sent him to them after all she'd said about them.

'Patsy wants to see you, love, and ... ' She continued with a guilt-ridden expression. 'I told Roy to tell her to come whenever she wants.'

Susie stared at her mum in shock. Patsy had the effrontery to want to see her after all her machinations to split their families up? Anger, frustration and heartbreak coursed through Susie. Now she'd got what she wanted, now the damage was done, how could Patsy think there was anything to say?

Susie shot up from the sofa.

'Well, I haven't anything to say to her!' Curtailing her sobs, Susie made for the door, 'The damage is done! No amount of talking will make amends for her behaviour!'

As she hurried along the hall however, there was a knock at the front door. Gwen came into the hall, but Susie cried out, 'Tell her I don't want to speak to her!'

'But you have to sort it before your wedding.'

There's not going to be a wedding! Susie inwardly screamed.

'I'll go and make a cup of tea and give you both time to sort things out,' Gwen said as she opened the front door.

Susie had little choice as Patsy stepped into the hall.

Seeing Susie, she murmured, 'I've

behaved badly, and I want to try and put things right, Susie. Once I've said my piece I'll go — and you need never speak to me again.'

'You better come in, then,' Susie said through gritted teeth.

What could Patsy say that would put things right? Nothing would ever be right again!

Patsy looked down at her hands.

'I've made some terrible mistakes, Susie, and I want to try and put some of them right.'

A myriad of questions raced through Susie's mind, wondering what her former friend could ever say to make all this mess right again.

'Tom Prand likes you — and he has all these crazy ideas about your shop and what he could do if he ran it,' she bagan, the words tumbling from her mouth. 'He said if I couldn't split you and Lex up he would get my dad sacked from his job! I didn't believe him so I told him I wouldn't do it, but then the next day Dad came home and said he'd had a verbal warning . . . '

She stifled a shuddering sob and went on, 'Tom was so full of himself, boasting to the gang about how he did something dishonest at work and pinned the blame on my dad and that Dad could get sacked if it happened again. They thought it was hilarious . . . ' Her voice trailed off as she wrung her hands together in her lap.

'I don't know what I ever saw in that lot now.' She shook her head. 'I was too enamoured of them all to see what they were truly like. And because Tom is so power-crazy he got them all complying with him by threatening them.'

As she paused, a blush ran up her neck. 'I'm ashamed to admit I had a bit of a crush on Tom in the beginning. Then he started threatening me, and I couldn't bear seeing my dad out of work again. It was so awful for him before the new gasworks took him on.'

She turned to Susie with her face full of pleading. 'I'm so sorry — really, I am! When it didn't end between you and Lex, Tom threatened to get Dad sacked, so I did everything he asked. I even . . . ' She sneaked a glance at Susie. 'Oh Susie, I can't tell you all the things I did! The things I said to make Lex think you didn't want him any more.'

Patsy's stricken expression turned Susie's anger into compassion.

'And now, because Lex is seeing you again, my dad had a second written warning at work today.'

Susie put her arm round Patsy's shoulder.

'Thank you for telling me all this, Patsy. But Tom has got to be stopped.'

Patsy trembled.

'How? If I expose him he says he'll tell everyone what I've done.'

Now Susie's compassion for Patsy curdled into fury at Tom!

'Did you intercept and give to Tom any letters between Lex and me?'

Appalled, Patsy stared at Susie in utter shock.

'No!'

Relief flooded through Susie.

'So he doesn't have any proof, does he? Patsy, it's his word against yours.'

Patsy groaned.

'But his stepdad is the foreman at the gasworks which means my dad will get sacked.'

15

Now that things made more sense, Susie knew not only that she wanted Patsy back as a friend, but that she also wanted to help her.

'Oh Patsy,' she whispered, 'if only I'd known what Tom was up to.'

Patsy trembled. 'Lex is mad about you, he never stopped loving you. This is all my fault — I'm so sorry!' She wrung her hands. 'Roy and I have talked it through again and again. They threatened him too, you know, but he wasn't having any of it! So the gang began giving things to his dad saying that Roy had stolen them. When he denied it, his dad hauled him back to the shops they'd stolen from and made Roy give the stuff back.'

'That's awful! Why is his dad so against him?'

'We think it's something to do with

him being a prisoner of war or shell-shock or something. He hasn't always been horrible to Roy. Roy remembers him being kind and funny once.

'Apparently after his bizarre performance at the police station on Monday, he's been strongly advised to go for some kind of treatment. Roy's mum said she couldn't bear it any longer.'

Her tone went quiet and solemn as she added, 'Roy and I are getting married.'

Suddenly Susie's own heartbreak hurtled back. She felt the lumps of barbed wire spiking her throat, her stomach churned, her head throbbed.

Irrespective of Patsy's distress and regret, irrespective of the terrible circumstances, irrespective of the horror of blackmail, the stark truth had to be faced! She had to confess what she'd heard!

'So were Lex and I,' she just about managed to say, trying not to dissolve into tears. Her voice hitched as she barely managed to add, 'But Gloria's pregnant.'

Saying it out loud caused her body to physically shiver with heartbreak.

Patsy's reaction was peculiar. She blinked briefly, then jumped up and tore from the front room and was out of their house before Susie could say any more!

Mum came into the room. 'What happened?'

Susie was visibly shaking, but her mind was made up now. 'Mum, there are some things you should know . . . '

After Susie had finally told her mum everything, Gwen held Susie in her arms.

'Oh, Susie. I'm so sorry this has happened.'

'But remember, except for Dad, you promised not to say anything to anyone until Lex has told me himself,' Susie pleaded.

Gwen sighed. 'I'm not sure I'll be able to prevent Bernie from going round there to give Lex a piece of his mind.'

'No, he mustn't! Please, Mum, stop him!'

Just then Bernie stuck put his head round the door. 'Stop me doing what?'

★   ★   ★

Susie wasn't sure how long she'd spent in bed. After telling her dad everything, he had insisted that a tot of brandy in hot water would do her good and help her sleep.

'No wonder you've been feeling rough, darling.' Although his tone was sympathetic and soothing she knew there was a quiet anger beneath his gentle façade.

'I'll get over him, Dad,' she assured him with more confidence than she felt. 'I have a business idea that involves the flat, and as I'm not going to be getting married any time soon, I'd like to start the ball rolling as soon as possible.'

He nodded as she outlined her idea.

'Party Plan is a new concept, Dad.' She knew that right now due to her distress, he wouldn't deny her anything. 'Actually — ' at this point her stomach coiled and knotted as if the barbed wire in her throat had pushed downwards into her abdomen, ' — it was Lex who mentioned how popular and successful the scheme is in the US.'

'It's taking off here, too,' Gwen ventured.

'I think it's an excellent idea.' Bernie looked briefly at Gwen, but Susie couldn't be sure if it was a look of caution, or relief. 'Your mum and I will help in any way we can.'

Now, hours later, brushing her hair from her face, Susie slipped out of bed, put on her knee-length dressing gown, and went downstairs.

She felt renewed somehow, as if a major transformation had taken place. She would never get over Lex, she knew that now. She would love him forever, but having decided to let him go, she had to move on.

As she crept past the sitting room,

she heard her parents chatting quietly. Not wanting to disturb them, she padded into the kitchen.

'Oh!' She stopped suddenly.

Swiftly clicking the cover of the kitchen clock back into place, Tom Prand swung to face her.

'I thought you were at your evening class on Wednesdays?' His tone was oddly accusing and there was something odd about his manner. 'I came in with the tea cups and saw the clock was wrong.'

He stared at her waiting for an explanation.

'I'm not well,' she replied sharply.

He looked her up and down. 'Nobody said.'

'You're nothing but a vile black-mailer, Tom Prand,' she hissed at him.

He didn't even flinch, just looked right through her. Then with an air of complete nonchalance he sidled past her. 'I'll see myself out.'

Gwen must have heard the door open and close because a second later, she came into the kitchen looking a bit sheepish.

'I'm sorry Tom was still here when you came down, love. Your dad wanted to send him packing, or at least confront him about his blackmailing, but for Patsy's sake I persuaded him not to.'

Susie's stomach knotted and churned. What had she done in telling them?

'We hope it gets sorted out soon because it'll be awful if Len loses his job,' Gwen went on. 'Your dad and I have discussed the situation and although you feel differently we feel we ought to go and see them as soon as possible. Len should know what's really going on at work.'

Gwen glanced at the clock. 'Goodness, is it that late already? It's time for our bedtime drink.'

Susie wanted to remind her mum that they'd only just had tea, but didn't bother.

'How are you feeling now anyway, love?'

'A bit better.' Susie looked at her mum and saw the worry etched into her features. She put her arms around her and hugged her tightly as she told her, 'Mum, it's going to hurt for a long time, I can't deny that. I still love him. But Lex has to do the right thing, and I have a life I need to get on with.'

Gwen shivered slightly in spite of her positive words. 'Yes.' She winced. 'He does, and you you're right — you must make a different life for yourself.' She pulled away from Susie.

'It's going to be all right. I promise,' Susie said with more conviction than she felt.

★   ★   ★

Susie sat bolt upright. Her heart was pounding and her head roared as the recurring nightmare reverberated through her brain.

In her dream it was dark, and she'd just locked up the shop while her mum popped up to the Rowes, and she was going round the back alley when Tom Prand assailed her in the dark.

'Come on, Susie.' He jostled her. 'Lover boy's ditched you, so how about giving me a chance?'

'I've told you before Tom, I'm not interested.'

The next thing she knew was, he was on the ground and she was opening their back gate and flying through it.

She could hear his voice, harsh and aggressive.

'You'll be sorry for that, Susie Cotting, just you wait and see! You made me look a chump in front of the others by turning me down before, and you're going to pay for that. I don't know how long I can keep my boys off, so everything that happens from now on is your fault!

'You can stop all this right now by agreeing to be my girl. You and your family think you're such bigwigs but you're nothing but small time, insignificant shopkeepers!'

Through the thick fog swirling in her

brain, something somehow told Susie that all this wasn't just a dream!

How could she have forgotten? How could she have put it so far out of her mind that it had became like a dream?

Tom hadn't just assaulted and threatened her in the alley, either — he'd also threatened her the day she walked away from the gang.

She had ignored him at the time, assuming he was making big-headed but idle threats. She shivered. What was Prand planning to do exactly? Recalling his words all over again made her tremble. What would she and her family be sorry for? And what about his vile treatment of Patsy and Len?

Her mind went back to seeing him in the kitchen earlier. What had he been doing? Was he altering their clock?

An inexplicable eerie feeling slid through her as she went through it second by second.

Then, checking her bedside clock she noted it was nearly two. Slipping out of bed, sliding her feet into her slippers and throwing on her dressing gown, she crept downstairs to the kitchen.

She was just being silly really, but she had to check the clock . . .

Turning on the light, she repressed a gasp. The clock was forty-five minutes fast. Had Prand altered it — and if so, why?

A sudden noise outside at the back of the shop made her jump. She stood still and listened. There was nothing. All was silent. Had she only imagined it?

Then there was another noise. This time it sounded like a lock being wrenched open!

The hairs on her spine rose as the horror of what might be happening engulfed her. Their shop was being raided!

Instinctively knowing she had to get to the shop before any damage was done, Susie unlocked the back door and was at the back of the shop before she'd even had time to think about what she was doing. The door was open, and she crept through. On reaching the kitchen she automatically stood still and listened. A sensation of complete calm floated through her as she tiptoed noiselessly into the shop.

She was still calm even when she flicked on the light and saw Tom Prand waving a now ineffective torch around while issuing orders to two other members of his gang.

All three instantaneously spun to stare at her. The astonishment on each face was almost amusing if it hadn't been for the seriousness of the situation. One of the gang, brandishing a crowbar above the glass counter, stopped waving, leaving it hanging in mid-air.

Tom recovered his senses first.

'Look who's come to join in the fun,' he sneered. 'Lover boy Lex not with you?'

The crowbar hovered dangerously over her mum's precious counter.

Susie's voice came out amazingly calm and firm. 'I suggest you all leave immediately.'

There were guffaws of laughter.

'You gonna to make us?' Tom scoffed.

Susie inwardly prepared herself . . .

Observe your adversary's waist or hips, not their hands or feet — this is more likely to reveal their specific purpose. Do not give anything away in your own stance, in your expression, or in your breathing . . .

'Yes.' Susie's tone was steady. 'If I have to.'

Prand suddenly rushed at her.

Dodging to one side Susie instantly repositioned herself by maintaining an upright posture, bending her knees slightly and placing one foot a little in front of the other.

There was a snigger of derision from one of the gang members. 'She thinks she can do martial arts!' he scoffed.

Catch your opponent coming in. Keep your eyes at waist level. Give the impression of total relaxation . . .

The second Tom reached her, Susie thrust a hand onto his shoulder.

Steadying her forward leg, she skipped deftly sideways. Then she brought her other leg up behind Tom's ankle and pushed his shoulder with her hand while yanking his ankle towards her.

Tom smashed painfully to the ground with a surprised grunt.

Another gang member moved towards her.

Without even having to think about it, Susie hunkered down slightly. As the gang member stooped, she rose up while he was off guard, zipped her right arm round his upper left arm, threw her right foot into position, turned sideways and yanked him over her shoulder before he even had time to react.

In seconds he too lay groaning on the floor.

'Put it down,' she said steadily to the gang member still wielding the crowbar.

He stared at her for a split second then sprang.

Susie raised her leg and thrust her foot hard into his solar plexus. Less than a second later, he'd joined his friend on the floor.

'What the devil's going on?'

Susie swung round to see the faces of her shocked parents.

'I'm fine,' she said. 'Call the police.'

★   ★   ★

By morning the shop, still being inspected by the police, was the focus of attention of the whole street and beyond. The press came, fingerprint experts arrived — and to Susie's surprise Lex and his family arrived with Roy.

'They know everything,' Lex announced as Susie let them into the house. 'The police went into the gasworks and explained to Magower what's been going on, so Dad's been given the day off. Patsy has to see her manager on Monday pending investigations.' He swallowed hard. 'And I've come to sort things out between us.'

As they all settled into the sitting

room, Susie rushed into the kitchen to make tea. She couldn't bear to hear how sorry Lex was, to see the look of guilt and sadness riding across his face!

Lex came into the kitchen behind her, however.

'Just leave it, Lex,' she snapped as she put the kettle on. 'It was a shock hearing Gloria announce her pregnancy in the burger bar, but I've accepted that we can't get married.'

'You overheard Gloria in the burger bar?'

'Yes.' Susie was determined to be strong! 'My class was cancelled, so I went there for a coffee before getting the bus home.'

'But Susie — '

'No, Lex. My mind is made up. I'm starting up a business instead. I have it all planned. I shall become what you so disparagingly call a career woman. So even if for some reason you reject the mother of your child, I shall — '

'No! That's not . . . '

Too upset to say any more, Lex's

voice trailed off as he folded his arms and frowned at Susie.

It had been bad enough hearing about Gloria's plight, and although his heart went out to her, it was extremely difficult telling her he wouldn't marry her. She'd been stunned at first, then outraged, threatening to tell everyone the child was his anyway. When he gently refused again, she began sobbing uncontrollably — as well she might under the circumstances.

At last he found his voice.

'Do you think so little of me that you believe I would have considered marrying you if there was the faintest chance another woman was expecting my baby?'

Determined not to capitulate in any way, Susie forced back her emotions and shrugged.

Lex looked at the set of her jaw, the suppressed emotion, and the glistening of repressed tears, and realised that, as heartbroken as he was that she seemed to think so little of him, she was suffering too.

'You heard a part of a conversation in the burger bar,' he told her softly, 'and immediately jumped to conclusions.' He drew a deep sigh. 'But I can assure you that the child Gloria is expecting is not mine.'

'You're denying it?'

'I don't need to deny it, Susie. Gloria knows, she told me herself. The father is a married man she was seeing before she met me.' He sighed. 'And she began seeing him again recently.'

Susie stared at him and saw his face a mask of pain.

'Surely you remember my reaction when you mentioned the word 'affair', Susie?'

How could she have misjudged him like this? And how could he still want to marry her after she had been so willing to think so badly of him?

He must have read her thoughts, because a slow sensual smile crossed his face.

'I want us to be together forever,

Susie — if you'll still have me, that is . . . '

'Oh Lex!' Ignoring the whistling kettle, Susie threw her arms round him. 'I'm so sorry for doubting you! Can you ever forgive me?'

'Of course I can, my darling.'

Seeing the longing in his eyes made every nerve in her body shimmy and dance with the thrill of knowing he still wanted her!

He whisked her into his arms. 'Oh, Susie,' he whispered as she tilted her chin up to him, bending to gently graze her mouth with his.

As his lips brushed hers her body slid into a silky softness, her spine shimmied, and her knees felt spongy.

'Ahem . . . ' Bernie coughed.

They pulled apart. 'I'm so sorry, Mr Cotting.'

Bernie laughed. 'No need to be, but I do need to take this kettle off the gas.'

Lex stood aside to let Bernie reach the kettle. 'By the way,' he said, 'what's all this about Susie saving the shop?'

Bernie chuckled and winked at Susie.

'Jujitsu,' he said with pride. 'Susie's been going to lessons every Wednesday night.'

'Jujitsu?' Lex gasped. 'You mean I'm marrying a martial arts expert as well as a fashion party-plan business woman?' Lex winked at Bernie. 'And who just so happens to have booked her first party for the day after we come back from honeymoon?'

Chuckling, Bernie grinned. 'You are indeed, Lex, you are indeed . . .'

Epilogue

It was the day of their wedding and as they lined up for photographs, Susie beamed up at Lex.

'Now that we're married we can we tell her together,' she said.

Lex grinned down at Susie, his spine tingling with the pleasure of them being together at last.

'Yes, our wedding day is the perfect time to put everything behind us,' he agreed.

They turned to Patsy in unison.

'Will you grant us a wish on our wedding day?'

Patsy, glowing in her dusky pink satin bridesmaid dress, beamed at them.

'Of course, I'll grant you anything on your wedding day.'

'We want you to stop apologising Patsy. It's finished and it's all in the past.'

'Yes,' Susie added, 'Tom and the gang are going to get what they deserve and we never want you to mention how sorry you are again. You're not just my very best friend, Patsy you're my sister-in-law now. We want you to forget it.'

Patsy sniffed a little through a smile. 'I promise,' she said.

She squeezed the hand of the young man next to her. 'Roy and I are grateful for everything your family has done, Susie.' She blushed. 'His window cleaning round is really taking off.'

Leaning forward, she tweaked Susie's veil. 'Perfect,' she grinned then leaning closer, she whispered, 'make sure you throw the bouquet in my direction!'

Susie giggled. 'Of course!'

As the photographer adjusted his lens, Lex raised one eyebrow. 'What was that about?'

That familiar habit of his made her head swirl and her knees tremble; all she could do was silently stare up at him.

'Let's have a toast!' Bernie broke the spell as the song *You are My Destiny* by Paul Anka faded.

Lex gave Susie a roguish grin as he stood to raise his glass.

'Here's to my beautiful career woman bride!'

He beamed with pride and before she could even prepare herself, he tipped her chin up and kissed her.

We do hope that you have enjoyed reading this large print book.

Did you know that all of our titles are available for purchase?

We publish a wide range of high quality large print books including:
Romances, Mysteries, Classics
General Fiction
Non Fiction and Westerns

Special interest titles available in large print are:
The Little Oxford Dictionary
Music Book, Song Book
Hymn Book, Service Book

Also available from us courtesy of Oxford University Press:
Young Readers' Dictionary
(large print edition)
Young Readers' Thesaurus
(large print edition)

For further information or a free brochure, please contact us at:
Ulverscroft Large Print Books Ltd.,
The Green, Bradgate Road, Anstey,
Leicester, LE7 7FU, England.
Tel: (00 44) 0116 236 4325
Fax: (00 44) 0116 234 0205

Other titles in the
Linford Romance Library:

SAVING ALICE

Gina Hollands

Naomi Graham is the best family lawyer in the country. But beneath her professional demeanour lies a broken heart. When the man who caused that heartache — billionaire ex-husband Toren Stirling — returns to her life after a ten-year absence, Naomi doesn't want to know. Their painful struggle to start a family tore their relationship apart, so when Toren reveals that he has a young daughter, Alice, it comes as a shocking blow. Not only that, but he's now fighting a custody battle — and needs Naomi's legal expertise to help him win.